A BLOOD BOOKS NOVEL

BLOOD MAGIC

DANIELLE ROSE

Blood Magic
A Blood Books Novel

Cover design by Wicked by Design
Editing by Narrative Ink Editing LLC
Book design by Inkstain Interior Book Designing

For my amazing readers—

BLOOD MAGIC

Jessica—

Never stop dreaming
your wildest dreams.
XO,

Danielle Rose

7-2016

CHAPTER
ONE

As a mortal witch destined to fight in a war against immortal vampires, my life had been surrounded by death. Before my birth rite, the ritual in which I obtained The Power, the ultimate weapon against the vampire race, I had even prepared for my own death. Being chosen came with consequences—likely not living to see my next birthday was one of them. I had accepted this fate, because my sacrifice would bring honor to my coven. Unfortunately, the prophecies were right. Obtaining The Power did result in my death—I became one of the creatures I had spent my life hunting.

I closed my eyes, focusing on my breathing. As a spirit user, I had a small affinity for all elements, but as a chosen one, a being who harnessed The Power, I had greater control. According to

Sebastian, the only other vampire I'd met who shared my differences, that control was limitless, but he had yet to show me how to wield the gift.

I called upon the element air. A breeze swirled around me, fluttering through the thick locks that hung past my shoulders. I smiled as it sent shivers down my spine. As a vampire, I didn't feel cold in the same way I had as a mortal, but I still felt the sensation, and it was uncontrollably overwhelming. With my new, heightened senses, I could feel everything around me. It was as if the blindfold had finally been lifted, and after years of living in darkness, and even in silence, I could finally see, could finally hear. I had to die to truly feel alive.

As I brushed my palm against the dead grass I sat atop, I admired my handy work. I had been carving protection runes into headstones for hours and was due for a break. I knew the sun would rise soon, and with it, the remaining members of my vampire coven would slumber. But first, there was much to be done. Seventeen vampires from my new coven had fallen, including the guards of our coven's high priestess, Amicia. Jasik, my sire, explained that a burial had never been rushed. In fact, we were skipping key parts, but with Amicia missing, we weren't given the luxury of something as simple as time.

No one would talk about the likelihood that she had also been killed. Instead, my fellow Hunters and I put saving Amicia at the top of our to-do list and then called it a day. Ignoring the fact that Amicia was probably already dead didn't bother me as much as it should have. Being a Hunter, a vampire blessed with my very own set of superpowers, it was my job to protect my coven and the members within it. We had failed when she was taken. Saving her was the only way to redemption.

Though I focused on carving the thick lines into the headstone, my eyes kept flickering to the vampire beside me. Sebastian had offered his help—a ploy, I was sure. Nearly four days had passed since I threatened to kill him if he didn't tell me everything I wanted to know. He had brushed off my crassness with ease. Even now, as I watched him, he ignored me.

Lingering thoughts crept their way back into my mind. I remembered the dream I had the night I discovered we'd won the battle but lost so many in exchange. The Sebastian in my dream was nothing like the one sitting beside me. In my dream, he was cruel, evil. I was sure it was a vision warning me of what was to come. Being a spirit user, I had visions, but I had yet to learn control. I shuddered at the memory of the Hunters hanging from a tree, split open from navel to neck, their innards swaying from side to side as they hung, lifeless. Had I influenced it in some way? Was Sebastian lying in wait? I shook my head to clear my mind. I needed to remain focused on the task at hand. With one final stroke, the rune was complete. I stood, sheathing my knife and wiping the fine shards of rock from my hands.

"How much longer?" I asked.

"Done," Sebastian replied as he stood, his light, sandy-brown hair bouncing as he moved. It fell to just below his chin. His lanky frame towered over my short stature, though he wasn't quite as tall as Jasik.

I nodded, glancing around. We were attacked in this very place. Rogues, soulless, evil vampires who feasted on the blood of the living, had attacked my witch coven the eve of my birth rite and left me for dead. When they realized they'd failed to truly kill me, they came back to finish the job. Though I escaped again, others died in my stead. I closed my eyes, listening to the wind rustle the leaves. I focused on them but felt nothing. The world was empty. Our coven was broken. I hadn't been a vampire for long, but I was already drawn to them. It was powerful, unexplainable. They felt like family—family I had failed to protect.

I opened my eyes, ignoring the cheeky grin plastered on Sebastian's face. He had been with us for almost four days, and he had already gotten on my nerves. He was always watching me—just as I was watching him. He liked watching me tap into this power within myself, and even though he wouldn't admit it, I believed he liked knowing it was always just out of reach. I think he felt safer that way. No one but me had the power to truly hurt him. He knew that. Jasik knew that. I knew that. And it left a gnawing sensation in the pit of my gut. I didn't like being bested, and I especially didn't like being vulnerable.

I turned on my heel and walked the stone path that led to the manor's front door. My new vampire coven was hidden deep within rural Washington State. The forests of national parks surrounded us, keeping our existence secret from prying eyes. Each evening, I woke to crashing ocean waves and thick, salted air. It was nothing like home. My family moved from the remote woodlands of Wisconsin to the mountains of Shasta, California nearly a decade ago. I missed home. I missed Wisconsin and Shasta. I missed my family. But they had turned their backs on me when I needed them most—and now it was my turn to walk away from them.

I glanced back at the cemetery that was laid before our manor's front entrance. Thinking about how cliché my new vampire life was put a smile on my face when times only called for sorrow. Our gothic manor, painted with splashes of gray and black, sat on wooded property in the middle of remote land, and our front yard consisted of a burial ground and mausoleums. Now all I needed to do was turn into a bat, fall in love with a human, renounce my new destiny, and call it a day. I chuckled at the thought.

"What's on your mind, love?" Sebastian asked, his Australian accent coating his words.

I rolled my eyes. "*Please* stop calling me that."

Sebastian frustrated me to no end, and though I didn't fully trust him, I found myself questioning myself more. It was easy to fall into step beside him. I allowed myself moments of peace even though he was within reaching distance. This was a mistake I never would have made as a human, a witch. Why now? Was it my knowledge of the power bubbling within me? Was it his easy-going personality? Why did he affect me like this?

I opened the front double doors, and Sebastian closed them behind us as we entered. Vampires lingered in the conservatory and smiled softly as I passed. I smiled back as I took the grand stairs two at a time. I wasn't sure what our relationship was. They were my family now, and I had accepted that—even though, at first, there had been a lack of trust on both parts. My survival was dependent on them, and it seemed, their survival was dependent on me. We both needed each other in ways we didn't understand.

The double doors to Amicia's office were open. With Sebastian by my side, I entered, nodded to my fellow Hunters, and made my way to her desk, where Jasik sat, flipping through pages of a thick book. Dark circles were painted below his eyes, and he ran a hand through tangled hair. We slept in shifts after Amicia's abduction, but I suspected Jasik skipped his rounds altogether.

I cleared my throat, and Jasik tore his eyes away from the yellowed paper to meet mine.

"Is it finished?" he asked.

"Yes. The runes are carved, and the headstones are spelled. We can begin the ceremony at any time," I answered.

He released a quick burst of air—no doubt the breath he'd been holding since Amicia had been taken. He leaned back in the chair, running his hands over his eyes.

"I've been reading Amicia's journals for days and haven't found anything," he said, dropping his arms and straightening in the chair. "I only know my part and the basics. But it's not enough. It's been too long since we've…" It was an odd feeling: we were thankful for the lack of deaths, but the distance between the last burial ritual and now meant no one could remember the exact steps that needed to be taken. No one but Amicia, that is.

"We do what we can," Malik said. He looked just as exhausted as his brother. I knew it had to be difficult for Malik to watch his younger brother in such pain, even though the hard features of his face betrayed nothing. I was always amazed by Malik's ability to be completely and thoroughly unreadable.

"That won't be enough," Jasik said.

"Maybe we can do something different this time. I've done countless burial ceremonies. I mean, it's the least I can do," I said, hopeful.

"As much as I hate to say it, she's right," Lillie said, her Irish accent faint. She was sitting beside Malik, her pixie blonde locks in disarray. Her usual bright, blue eyes were red, puffy. We hadn't always seen eye-to-eye, but her confession didn't surprise me. We really didn't have another option. There were thousands upon thousands of hand-written journals in Amicia's library. After all, she was over seven hundred years old. A girl could accrue a lot of crap in that amount of time.

"I agree," Jeremiah said. I almost hadn't noticed him. Even now, he cowered in the corner, hiding in the shadows. "Besides, we need to get this over with." The harshness of his words struck anger in the others' eyes.

"Jeremiah—"

"I didn't mean—I just meant we need to hurry. The longer Amicia's out there, the more likely she's going to die. We just need to hurry and get her back, and then things can get back to normal."

"I don't think anything will ever be normal again," I said, meeting Jeremiah's sad, gray eyes. His dark chocolate skin turned ashy as he nervously scratched at his arms.

No one spoke. I knew we were all thinking the same thing: we couldn't go back to what we had. We had to move on, to let go. Opening our arms to the future and its possibilities was harder than we imagined.

"Okay. Avah will lead the burial, but it needs to be done tonight."

I nodded. "Everything I need should be in the basement stock room." I glanced at the clock. Still four hours before dawn. Plenty of time. "I just need an hour."

"We'll make the announcement while you prepare, then."

I left Amicia's office in a daze. Jasik rarely spoke of vampire law to me. In fact, my only experience with it had been when he had broken it to change me. I was on the brink of death, and I suppose he thought the sacrifice was worth it. The cost, he had explained, was death. Thankfully, Amicia granted him immunity. The day following Amicia's capture, Jasik had explained just how important it was to find Amicia: the Hunter's sole purpose was to protect his priestess. Failure would cost the Hunter his life. Bringing Amicia home, alive, was our only option.

I entered the basement quarters with Sebastian tailing me. It was easy to forget he was around—especially during the rare occasions he chose to remain silent. He was stealthy, invisible... almost.

"I don't need assistance," I said without meeting his gaze. I didn't like the power he held over us. He had information about what I was, and he had the strength that we could have used in battle. He had saved me, and I was grateful, but still, I couldn't stop thinking of 'what-ifs.' What if he had gotten there sooner? What if he had bypassed me and saved the others? What if...

"You sure? I've been to my fair share of burials, too." He quickened his pace so he was walking beside me.

I swung the door to our stock room open and walked inside. I discovered this room a few weeks ago, and it had become difficult to stay away. In it, we stored all things magical: relics, herbs, powders, oils, crystals, candles, books, and more. I remembered my first reaction to this room wasn't as pleasant. The elders of my witch coven had taught me that vampires and witches could—and would—never find a common ground. But since I became a vampire, that's all I've seemed to discover: a common ground.

"Want to help? Here," I said, grabbing some items from a shelf and tossing them into his arms. "Hold these." I grabbed the final pieces for our burial ritual and closed the door behind me.

Outside, I sat the items down beside the cemetery and began to work my magic—literally. The hour I spent cleansing ritual relics by passing them through the sage stick's smoke and setting up for circle seemed to come to an end almost as soon as it began. Behind me, black-clad members of my coven filed out of the manor and took the steps down toward me.

I smiled at my house-mates. "I know this isn't going to be the ceremony you're used to, but I promise I will do my best to honor our fallen. It is very important that you do not cross this line," I said, pointing to an invisible barrier. In truth, there was nothing there, but I couldn't allow anyone to break the circle. Had I had the time to learn control, I would have raised my own shield—one of my nifty vampire powers—as a barrier. "Sebastian will cleanse my aura and then join you."

I nodded to Sebastian, and he stepped forward, grabbing the burning bundle of sage. While I didn't fully trust his motives for finding me, I knew I didn't have another choice. Only a witch could speak these words, and besides me, he was the only one around.

"How do you enter?" he asked.

"With perfect love and perfect trust," I said. He waved the smoke stick up and down the length of my body. I turned so my back faced him, and he repeated the cleansing motion. I entered the circle, picked up my athame dagger, pressed the tip to the ground, and closed the circle. I walked to the center, where my altar sat. On it, I placed relics to represent each of our seventeen fallen members. Jasik and the other Hunters had chosen their memorial items. They brought pictures, cherished collectibles, and more.

I took a deep breath, calming the turmoil that raged within me, and then faced east. With my arm outstretched, I maintained my grasp on the athame and pointed the tip before me and toward the sky. "All that falls must rise again, and so, our friend shall be reborn. The treasure of life is the air we breathe, that for which we will forever be grateful. I call to the gods of the east to bless this circle."

Still holding the athame, I turned and faced south. "As our life is but a day, our friend has passed into the night. Our strength, memories, courage, and the fires of our lives are given to us by our fallen friend. I call to the gods of the south to bless this circle."

The athame burned in my hand now as the power of my words fueled its energy. I turned again, this time facing west, and said, "As the sun sets, our friend has now left us. Our tears are like the waters of the ocean. I call to the gods of the west to bless this circle."

One final time, I turned and faced north. "As the earth has formed us, we now must return our friend back to that earth. We honor the gods for the life they have bestowed upon us and our friend. I call to the gods of the north to bless this circle."

My breath came in short, quick bursts, as the elements swirled around and within me. As they flowed into each crevice of my being, I smiled and silently thanked the gods. I may not have been a very good vampire, but I was a damn good witch.

I turned to face the altar and the remaining members of my coven, who watched with watery, wide eyes.

I raised the athame and pointed it toward the moon, saying, "You are the moon, Mother Earth, and the goddesses. Though you have fallen, you will remain an eternal creation, a life with no end, a never-ending cycle.

"You are the sun, the gods. You are born from us and will live through us. You only live and die to be reborn again. You are the destroyer, the ruler of the land of the dead.

"Bless our friends and see them safely into Summerland, where they will await their rebirth. May they be reborn again at the same time as the ones they have loved now, so they may know and love them again." With a final thrust, I twirled the athame in my hand and stabbed it into the cold, hard ground.

I stepped away from the athame, leaving it handle-deep in Mother Earth. I tore my teary eyes from the crowd and glanced at the seventeen candles standing tall on my altar.

"*Incendia*," I said, calling to fire. In unison, the seventeen candles sparked, their wicks igniting in flame.

"Though the wick on these candles will burn, the eternal fires within our hearts will never die. We say goodnight and goodbye to our fallen family, as they now must pass through Summerland with the knowledge that they will be missed and forever remembered in our thoughts and hearts. Blessed be, our friends, our family. May your crossing be peaceful and swift."

I grasped the handle of the athame and focused on its energies. The gods heard my plea and accepted our offering. The athame's handle, once burning with the power and energy I had left in it, now felt empty, a sign of acceptance. I pulled the athame from the ground, ending the ceremony. I set the athame on the altar and slowly raised my gaze. The others smiled at me with hopeful eyes.

One by one, the vampires walked to the graves to pay their respects. Most cried, and I found myself wondering just how long our fallen had been part of this coven's life. Had they been here since the beginning? Or were they newborns, their lives cut short by the burden of war? I was lost in my thoughts and hadn't heard Jasik approach from behind.

"That was beautiful," he said, pulling me toward him. I fell against his frame, resting my head against his chest. I closed my eyes and listened for his slow, steady heartbeat. The sound had been shocking when I first changed. I hadn't expected to find a heart, but I discovered that vampires had so much more than just beating hearts: like mortals, they had souls, desires, and downfalls. I opened my eyes to find Malik beside me, staring curiously.

"I was hesitant, but you came through. Thank you," he said before walking away, joining the other Hunters in the manor. Malik was very slowly opening up to me, and though I knew he needed time to accept the fact that his brother broke a vampire law of utmost importance by changing me, I still wanted him to just let it go. We had more important things to worry about, but had I said that to him, he'd probably simply tell me my ignorance betrayed my youth.

I stepped away from Jasik and wrapped my arms around my chest, watching as each vampire placed his or her hand atop a tombstone and spoke just above a whisper. They prayed that their loved ones would find their way home, and then they went inside, leaving their graves behind to seek shelter and comfort wherever they could find it.

"Sebastian refueled the protection spells around the manor," I said as I walked toward the front gate. "I just want to make a quick perimeter run to be sure everything's okay."

"I'll join you," Jasik said, grabbing onto my hand as we left the safety of the magical shield that kept Rogues from entering the manor while we slumbered.

Our manor was enclosed within a black wrought-iron fence

boundary, and at each of the four corners, I had placed power-infused crystals to protect us. As we passed each now, I could feel its strength, power radiating from its points. Sebastian hadn't failed me. I wondered if I should consider giving him the benefit of the doubt.

"What's on your mind?" Jasik asked. I glanced up to find him staring at me intently.

"Nothing, really. Just thinking about everything—Amicia getting back, Sebastian and his many secrets."

"We need to discuss what we are to do," Jasik said, nodding.

"I think... I think he needs to join us when we begin tracking Amicia," I said.

Jasik came to an abrupt stop, turned, and faced me. I knew he wasn't going to like my suggestion.

"I think he'll be useful. We can keep an eye on him, and he and I can work one on one."

"Avah, it's not safe. We can't trust him. Not yet."

"If he wanted to kill me, don't you think he would have tried by now? Something? Anything?" It was true that I had lingering doubts regarding Sebastian's intentions, but admitting so would only fuel the fire Jasik was kindling. But I also couldn't deny that my faith in him held a stronger pull than my doubt. When it came to the unreadable Sebastian, I was left a mess of emotions.

"Not when he's facing a house full of vampires, an experienced team of Hunters, and you, but when we leave, it'll just be us. We'll be busy tracking, and you'll be alone with him."

"I don't need you to protect me, Jasik. I need to figure this out by myself."

Pain flashed in his eyes, and I immediately regretted my words.

"Jasik," I said, reaching for him, my fingertips lightly brushing against his skin, "I didn't mean it like that. I just need to figure this out, and I'd like answers sooner rather than later. Besides, we can't just leave him at the house alone, unprotected. This isn't like your usual hunts. We'll be gone for weeks, not hours or days. They'll be too vulnerable."

"I've already contacted other covens. Each house is willing to send one Hunter here for protection. Our coven will be safe. The other Hunters will watch over him, ensuring he doesn't do anything he'll regret when we return."

"And you need to trust that *I* will be fine. I can do this. I can handle Sebastian. I can protect myself."

"Not against him. We still don't know his true power," Jasik said.

"But more importantly, we still don't know *my* power, and that's what matters. Besides, you won't need me to help you with tracking. I'll just be tagging along, really. So bringing Sebastian will give me something to do."

"Give you something to do? You speak as though saving Amicia isn't important to you."

I groaned and turned away but was caught by Jasik's hand. I yanked my arm free. "You *know* that's not what I meant. Of course she's important to me, but *she* doesn't need me. *I* need me."

"I need you, too," he said, looking away.

In my frustration, I hadn't realized just how important this was to him. Sure, he wanted to protect me, but he was vulnerable, too. He had failed in his duties to protect his high priestess. His wounded pride needed tending. I just couldn't give him that. Not when I couldn't trust the growing, uncontrollable power inside me.

"I care a great deal about Amicia. You know this. Don't belittle my feelings just because I want to spend my days training with Sebastian while you four track her. I'll still be there. I'll still be with you. And I'll help whenever you need me. But I also need to think about myself. While I'm being there for everyone else, no one is being there for me, and I—"

He scoffed and turned away. "You can't be serious, Avah! Do you truly believe no one is here for you? Every vampire in that house," he said as he flung his arm toward the manor, "is here for you. They all trust you. They all want you to be part of this coven, and being part of this coven means doing your job as a Hunter. There will be plenty of time for training, but our first priority must be Amicia's return."

I was shocked into silence. Sure, I was being selfish, but after everything we'd been through, *couldn't* I be selfish for once in my life?

"Jasik, what's really going on? You know this coven has become one of my top priorities."

He ran a hand through his hair and exhaled deeply. "I just don't trust him. I just—I just want you to do this my way. I don't want to question your safety, and I don't want to worry about Sebastian. Not right now."

I understood completely. Though he didn't say the words, I knew where his hurt lay. Sebastian was the first vampire we'd encountered who shared my differences. Hell, he could be the *only* other one in existence. I was sure that bothered Jasik more than he let on.

I wrapped my arms around his neck. "You know my decision to bring him along is because I need to learn more about who I am and what I can do. Nothing more, and nothing less."

"And what happens once you've learned everything he can teach you?"

I shrugged, pulling him closer. "Sebastian will go back to

Australia?"

Jasik closed his eyes and rested his forehead against mine. "When he's near… Everything feels different."

"What does that mean?" I whispered.

He shook his head. "I just… I don't know."

"Are you saying *you* feel differently for… for me?"

His eyes opened as he pulled away, and pain lingered there. "No. Of course not."

I nodded. His hand grasped mine, and he pulled me toward him. My mouth found his, and I leaned against him. Our bodies fit perfectly—each and every curve tucked neatly together. Hours could have passed before we finally pulled away breathlessly. I smiled up at him, his earlier unease gone.

"You're sure you can handle him?" he asked.

"Positive. I really think he doesn't want to hurt us."

"And if he does?"

I exhaled slowly, letting his words sink in. "If he does, well, then I'll take care of the situation."

While my instincts were telling me I could trust Sebastian, I couldn't deny the possibility that they'd betray me.

CHAPTER TWO

After my almost-tiff with Jasik, I went in search of Sebastian. The details describing just how we were supposed to find and save Amicia had already been decided, and plans were drawn out by the time Sebastian and I made our way into Amicia's office to meet with the other Hunters.

"Sebastian and I will be joining you," I said. I was eternally grateful to know that Jasik not only trusted me enough to let Sebastian join us, but he was also willing to set aside his leader tendencies and let me make my own decisions.

"We're what? I don't think so. I didn't come all this way to fight, sweet thing. Sebastian is staying here—where there are comfy beds, food to eat, and bathrooms. I don't do the whole *nature thing*." Sebastian referring to himself in the third person put the strawberry icing on the damn cake he'd been baking all day.

"That doesn't surprise me," Jasik said.

I held back a chuckle and said, "They need me. Amicia needs me, and I need you. So you're coming." I hoped my tone conveyed just how serious I was. We didn't have time to argue.

"How do you expect me to train you while you're tracking?"

"I don't need to track. I just need to be there when it's time to fight. While they track," I said, pointing to Amicia's Hunters, "you and I will train. Maybe you can teach me enough to make a difference by the time we find her."

"This isn't a good idea," Sebastian said. His tone was serious, and I found myself wondering if leaving was the wrong decision. It was so easy for him to make me second-guess myself. I'd trusted and leaned on my instincts for years while hunting vampires. They never failed me. But as soon as Sebastian opened his mouth, I was falling in step—in *his* step. I didn't like it.

"I second that. How do we know we can even trust him?" Lillie asked.

"But you're trusting enough to leave me here with the vampires you're meant to protect? You didn't think that one through did you, blondie?" Sebastian said. I rolled my eyes and met his gaze. I gave him my best *don't-tempt-her* glare before glancing past him. Amicia's office had large bay windows behind her desk. The manor was built on the far edge of a cliff that hung over the crashing Pacific Ocean. Slowly, the sky was lightening as the sun began to rise. If we were to leave tomorrow at dusk, then we needed plans set in stone quickly.

"Actually, I just thought we could lock you up until we get back and deal with you then," Lillie replied in her Miss America tone. She flashed him a wide smile.

"We're not doing that. Besides, I've been thinking about a locating spell, and to make it work, I'll need Sebastian's help." I ignored Sebastian's frown.

"Do you really expect a tracking spell to work? They know you're part witch. Don't you think the Rogues thought you might do that?" Lillie asked.

I nodded. "But it's worth a try. So are you going to come willingly, or am I going to have to convince you?" I said, placing my hand on my sheathed weapon. I realized too soon that I was joking, and an uncomfortable feeling settled. Since when did Sebastian and I get on joking terms?

Sebastian barked out a hard laugh. "I love your enthusiasm, Avah. You act as though you really could take me. It's going to make you a fantastic asset."

I rolled my eyes and turned back toward the others. "So what're the plans?"

"There are four Hunters arriving just after sundown. Tonight, we rest and feast. Tomorrow, we hunt, and we don't stop until we've found her," Jasik said as he stood. He closed the journal and slid it back into its place on Amicia's bookshelf. The room was spotless. You couldn't even tell that we'd been ransacking the place in the hopes of finding answers.

"We should get ready, then," Lillie said.

"Yes, go to the armory and replace our weapons. Clean and sharpen the ones we cannot leave behind. When done, deliver them to our rooms, and then everyone needs to feed and sleep. We have a long day tomorrow," Jasik replied. Especially since we were racing the sun...

"Do we have any idea where we're going?" I asked.

"We're heading east. I assumed your old coven would have contacted you if they went south. We have friends toward the east, too. If we make it to them, we'll have a safe place to rest and feed."

I nodded. Jasik made it sound so simple. I was sure it was anything but.

Jasik closed the meeting, staying behind to speak with Malik, and we dispersed. Sebastian and I went to the kitchen, grabbed bags of blood, and feasted until our stretched stomachs ached.

"So when are we going to begin these promised lessons?" I asked.

"Lesson number one: consider a different diet."

"Huh?"

"Let me backtrack. First, I need you to promise you won't run and tell lover boy everything I tell you. Some things are better left a mystery."

"You know I can't promise that."

"At least consider it. Trust me."

I thought before responding. Obviously, he knew things I needed to know, and he wasn't going to give it up without a few conditions being met. "Fine."

"Good. Back to lesson number one," he said, leaning in closely as if someone were attempting to eavesdrop. "We can eat *real* food."

My stomach, now full from blood, grumbled at the thought of munching on candy, devouring a plate of pasta, and sipping on sweet tea.

"We're… like a hybrid species. We have all the perks of both with none of the weaknesses. Well, close to none. We're not invincible. Cut our heads off, and another isn't growin' back."

"So we can survive *without* feeding?" Though the thought of never needing to drink blood again made me want to shriek in excitement, I found myself wondering what that would really mean. Jasik had been questioning my vampirism since I turned. Maybe he had been right the whole time.

"Sure can. I only drink blood when I'm around covens like this. Those who don't know any better. I like to keep up the mystique."

"Why does that not surprise me?" I grinned, shaking my head.

He chuckled and swallowed down the last swig of blood in his blood bag, making dramatic refreshing noises. I couldn't help but laugh. The unease began to sink back in, and I decided then and there that I'd give him a chance. He was keeping his promises, and though he put up a fight when I'd told him he was joining us on the hunt, he was going to help find Amicia. I'd never been in the position to lend trust to someone I didn't know. At least, not until I turned. Becoming a vampire had me questioning everything I thought I knew and everything I thought I was. Why not continue with giving him a chance? If I was wrong, it'd only cost me my life…

"I like you, Sebastian. Please don't make me regret that."

He winked at me. "I knew you couldn't resist my Aussie charm."

"I'm serious. This isn't a joke. Lives are at stake." I ignored his laugh at my unintentional pun. "And I'm going to need your help while we search for Amicia. I just need to know that I can count on you. You've shown me a different side of yourself since you initially arrived, and I want to make sure *that's* the Sebastian accompanying us on this venture."

"Relax, sweets. That's the only Sebastian I know. 'Sides, I do believe *you* were the one who was on the cranky side. Everyone seems to keep forgetting that *I* tried to *help* y'all."

"I know," I said, thinking back to the dream I had about Sebastian the night he arrived. I hoped it was anxiety and nothing more—especially since being around him was so easy, so natural. Briefly, I wondered what it would be like to have him join our coven. He'd definitely get along with Jeremiah if he were just given the chance.

When I met Sebastian's eyes again, his stare was cold, harsh. He blinked, and it was gone. His annoying cheerfulness returned with a wink. I fought the urge to ask what had just happened, where his mind had just gone.

"I'm getting tired. Let's pack for our spells and then hit the sack," I said.

"Sounds like a plan, my little blueberry muffin." I was sure he had just resisted the urge to pinch my cheeks.

"I think I just swallowed vomit."

"The best part of being a vampire is the liquid diet. It tastes even better going down a second time," he said as he bent over in silent laughter, as if he was just way too funny to handle.

"You're disgusting," I said, but inside, I told myself I could get used to this. I could get used to Sebastian's bad jokes and awful pet names. I wasn't sure if I should be thrilled or horrified.

Back in my room, I quickly showered and threw on a clean pair of underwear. I smiled when I saw Jasik fast asleep on the bed. His dark hair was sleep-fussed, and his sculpted facial features left me licking my lips at the sight of him. Slowly, I crept over and slid in beside to him. He was nude, and his skin burned against mine. I didn't understand the allure he had over me, and honestly, I didn't care. I yanked the sheet back and admired him. His tanned skin was taut against his tall, muscular frame. I rolled on top of him, my legs astride, and rested my bare chest against his, as I softly kissed his neck. He moaned but remained sleeping. I no doubt had just gotten a starring role in whatever he was dreaming.

I sank my fangs into his neck, and his hands grasped my waist. His breath came in quick bursts as he grabbed onto the back of my head, tangling his fingers in my damp hair. He was grinding against me, hardening against my leg, and he held me tightly, pulling me closer as I drank from him. He tasted as sweet as candy, and I knew I could drink until he shriveled into nothing. I pulled myself away, a drip of blood sliding down the curve of my jaw and onto my chest. He leaned forward and began kissing the crimson trail down my chin. His tongue generously teased my skin as he made his way to my chest. Carefully, he began teasing my nipple until it hardened and lengthened in response. I moaned, grasping his head with my hands, exploring his hair with my fingers. I lightly pulled on his hair as I pushed him closer to me, and he furiously kissed my body in return. I felt him below me, hardening, lengthening. When I could no longer bear the sensation, I cried out to him. "Jasik, please." My fangs were throbbing now, begging me to explore him further.

In a swift motion, he was on top of me, trailing kisses down the length of my torso. When he reached my inner thigh, he looked up at me, meeting my gaze, his eyes burning a bright, neon blue, a showcase of his arousal. I bit my lower lip, dragging my teeth across the skin, knowing it would drive him mad. His hand wrapped around my frame, grasping my bottom fiercely. I inhaled sharply as he began kneading my skin, pushing me against his hardened limb. I grabbed onto his arms, running my fingers along his flexed muscles as he pushed me faster, harder against him. I felt the familiar sensation build within me, and I knew I was close. My body tensed, and he released me.

Angrily, I leaned against my elbows, staring down at him. A mischievous grin plastered across his face before he sank his fangs into my inner thigh, and I fought to control the pleasure erupting within me. I threw my head back and collapsed against the bed;

my fangs lengthened again, their need making my entire body quiver. I felt his fingers lightly tease my skin just before he ripped my panties from me, the fabric falling to pieces as he tossed them to the floor.

Slowly, he inserted his index finger into me, and I writhed in response.

"Stay still, love. I want you to feel *everything* I'm going to do to you tonight." His words alone were enough to push me to the brink; I knew I couldn't hold on much longer.

He carefully inserted another finger and then pressed his palm against me, rubbing my sensitive nub as he pushed in and out, in and out. I cried out as I clenched around his fingers, unable to contain the ecstasy any longer. He waited, plunging deeper, sucking harder, as I rode the orgasmic wave, until my heavy-lidded gaze met his eyes. He withdrew from me and slowly crawled up the bed, his arms on either side of me, stopping when his mouth reached mine. My tongue lightly licked the blood that trickled at the corner of his mouth. I tasted *good.* The thought shocked me. I pulled him into a deep, hard kiss. He met my kiss with equal ferocity. I dipped my tongue in to meet his, grazing past, exploring. He tasted better than anything I'd ever enjoyed. God, I wanted this man, and nothing could keep us apart. Nothing.

I pulled back, breathless. "Where have you been all my life?"

The words escaped my lips before I'd even made the decision to speak them.

"Waiting for you…" he said fervently.

My breath caught. I had never loved anyone as much as I loved Jasik. Our love was new, inescapable. We'd fallen for each other almost as quickly as the gods had written it in our destinies. Our years of focus on the war left us inexperienced in love, but when he held me, I knew there was no place else I was meant to be. We fell fast, hard, because we were made to love each other.

I twisted so I was on top. I pressed a quick kiss to his lips and then angled my hips so that he easily slid into me. He closed his eyes, grasping my hips and moaning in response. Thick, long, and hard as stone, he filled me completely as I moved, slowly at first, up and down, taking pleasure in watching him squirm beneath me. Giving in, I quickened my pace until I had to grab the headboard to steady my movements. In unison, we lost ourselves in each other, our bodies shaking, sleek with dew.

I collapsed beside him and bit my lower lip. I could still feel the slickness of him within me, and the thought nearly drove me mad. I curved against him, gazing up at him with wanting eyes. I smiled wickedly and teased the skin around his navel with my fingertip.

"You, Milady, are insatiable," he said, staring at my taunting mouth.

I turned so that my head rested against his shoulder and inhaled deeply, taking in his scent. He smelled of sweat and blood and his own unique musk. It was intoxicating, and I knew I could take him again. Now. And he wouldn't stop me. We'd lose ourselves in each other if we could—if we could see past the responsibilities plaguing us.

"I think I'm going to take a walk," I said, sitting up, suddenly needing air—and to get my libido in check.

He nodded. "Be careful. Sun." He spoke sleepily and just above a whisper.

I smiled at him as I cleaned myself and dressed. By the time I opened the bedroom door to leave, he was in a deep sleep.

<hr>

"Can't sleep, sugar lips?" Sebastian said as I walked into the downstairs parlor.

"Seriously? Sugar lips?" I said, shaking my head as I took a seat beside him. "What are you doing in here?" It was nearly dawn, so the vampires of the house had long been asleep.

"I like it here. It's quiet during this time of day. No one to stare or ask questions. It's *almost* as close to peaceful as we can get."

"Almost?"

A sly grin formed. "Ready for lesson number fifteen?"

"Fifteen? I think we skipped a couple—"

"Nonsense," he said, waving a hand. "I'm a fantastic mentor. You're getting the best damn education money can buy."

"I'm not paying you, Sebastian," I said.

"Tsk. Tsk." He wiggled his finger at me. "Details. We'll cover those later. So?"

"Let's move on to lesson *fifteen*." I rolled my eyes and held back my chuckle.

His sly grin molded into a full-on cheeky smile as he stood, grabbed my arm, and yanked me out the front door. He stood behind me, covering my eyes with his hands.

"Sebastian, what are you doing? It's almost sunrise!"

His lips brushed the back of my ear, sending shivers down my body, and he whispered, "Not almost." My heartbeat increased, echoing almost painfully in my mind as I considered his words.

As he lowered his hands, his fingertips lightly brushed against the curve of my jawline. I opened my eyes quickly, without hesitation, but was blinded. I brought my hands up instinctively, and as my eyes adjusted to the light, I removed their cover. I kept my hands before me, staring at my palms. The heat from the sun that blared down upon us was so warm, so comforting. I felt like

I was back home in Wisconsin, sitting beside a fireplace as my father told me stories of the demons that walked in the night. I thought I'd never see the sun again.

"How is this—"

"Possible?" Sebastian said. "All things are possible now, Avah."

"It feels—"

"Amazing? Like nothing you've ever felt before?"

I nodded, my breath quickening. My heart was beating rapidly. I closed my eyes and listened. The creatures that embraced the night were long gone, sleeping in their beds, no doubt. The world was filled with new sounds from creatures I had forgotten. Birds chirped, squirrels ran through the forest, and deer pranced through the brush. The beauty of the world had been just out of reach for so long.

"The beauty of the world is never out of reach, Avah," Sebastian said, and my eyes shot open.

"How..."

"Look deep within you. You already know." He stepped closer, eliminating what little space was between us. I was acutely aware of his proximity. My hair seemed to stand on end.

"We have them all, don't we? All the Hunters powers?" I said.

"We do," was all he said.

When Sebastian arrived, his first instinct was to save my life, while mine was to put up walls, become defensive. I was overly cautious, as I had been trained to be around vampires. After settling for a day, and after allowing myself to feel more at ease around him, I had asked him what brought him here. His answer was simple.

"You brought me here, Avah," he had said.

"How?" I had asked, but he simply smiled and walked away, leaving me a confused mess. I didn't chase him and demand for an answer, because I was too afraid of what it might be, now, his words hung over me.

"Sebastian?" I asked.

"Hmm?" His eyes burned with hunger.

I swallowed the lump in my throat and asked, "What brought you here?"

His mouth curved into a small smile. "You."

I shook my head. "What does that mean?"

"One day, I woke, and all I could see was you. Your face haunted my days, my nights, my dreams... Whenever I'd glance into my future, I'd see you smiling back at me. I knew I had to find you. I had to find the girl who took my breath away every time she looked at me, every time she smiled my way, every time laughed. I was meant to find you, to be here with you."

My breath caught at his admission. I couldn't deny that there was something lingering between us. I didn't understand it, but I knew he was right: he was meant to find me, to be here with me.

He placed a finger below my chin, raising my head so that I met his gaze, and then he leaned down and brushed his lips against mine. I pulled away.

"What are you doing?" I said, stepping back. "I'm involved. You know that."

"Can't blame me for trying, right?" he asked with a boyish grin.

Frustrated, I moved farther away. I rested against the railing, crossing my arms over my chest as I stared at the sun. So much had happened: I learned the sun wasn't a threat, I confirmed I had all Hunter abilities, and I discovered that I was somehow part of Sebastian's future.

"I can't believe you did that," I whispered. In actuality, it didn't surprise me that he made a move. But did he have to choose the worst possible moment to do it? I closed my eyes, allowing myself to bask in the sun. Its warmth covered me in waves. "You took this moment from me—a moment I've wanted since I turned. How could you? Now every time I remember the day I re-experienced the sun—"

"You'll think of me."

I groaned and opened my eyes, pushing past him. "I'm going to bed, and don't even think of making a surprise visit. I'll stake you before you can even make a move," I yelled over my shoulder.

I retreated to the sounds of his low chuckle.

CHAPTER
THREE

Jasik's fingers softly traced the curve of my jawline. His velvety touch was smooth and sent shivers down my spine.

"I know you're awake," he said softly. He leaned in and brushed the tip of his nose against my cheek. "You can't fool me."

I opened my eyes, grinning, and rested my forehead against his chest. I kissed the skin there, tracing my fingers against the curves of his muscular torso.

"Good morning," I said, meeting his gaze. Jasik was gorgeous in a god-like way. He was so tall—at least six-five or so—with dark brown hair and bright, icy-blue eyes. Now, they mirrored my hunger, my desperation. I yearned for him and he for me. His hair sat messily atop his head, and I reached up, running my fingers through his silky locks.

"Good *evening*," he said with a small kiss against my lips, his British accent coating his words.

"What time is it?"

"Time to awaken. Company arrives within the hour."

I jolted out of bed. An hour? But there was still so much to do.

"Relax, Avah. I've handled everything. You just need to get ready and feed. Are you hungry?"

I bit my lower lip and nodded. "For more than just food..."

His eyes sparked to life. "You're quite the tease," he said, and in a blink, he was before me, tucking a loose strand of hair behind my ear. This vamp speed was alluring. As a witch, a mortal, it had never occurred to me to use my magic for personal gain, but now, as a vampire, all I could think about was who could rip the other's clothes off faster.

I smiled up at him, throwing my arms around his neck.

"As much as I'd like to take you to bed, I mustn't. We haven't the time. But soon," he promised. And with another quick kiss, he stepped back.

I groaned in response. I knew these next—days? weeks?—were going to be difficult, and I wanted nothing more than to crawl into his bed and forget about this war. The selfish part of me hoped he wanted that, too.

"Come. They'll be here soon."

As we cleaned and dressed, I remembered my unpleasant encounter with Sebastian. I felt my anger boil within me. He was unbelievably frustrating. Did he really think he had a chance with me? The only positive thing from our encounter was the sun. I closed my eyes as I pulled my hair back into a tight bun, reveling in the feeling of the heat as it burned against my skin—and it had only been dawn. What would it have felt like to watch the sun completely rise? To stand below its rays during its highest point? What would it have been like to watch it sink below the horizon and stand by as night engulfed the world?

I opened my eyes and found Jasik watching me carefully. Should I tell him? Yes, but when? My gaze moved from Jasik to the artwork on his bedroom walls. The pictures were of various scenery: cityscapes, flatlands, hills, mountains. Their landscapes had but one common theme: the sun. How did you tell someone who could never experience the sun again that you could? How could I tell him his fondest memory from mortality would be my reality? I distracted myself with thoughts of the other Hunters. I had seen some at the masquerade ball, but few spoke to me. At that time, they didn't know if they could trust me yet. Now that it was obvious, I wondered how different our interactions would be.

"If only I could be a reader," Jasik said, and I lost my train of thought. We had long suspected that I had the ability to tap into all four of the vampire powers—something only hybrids could do—the ability to read someone's mind was one of them. Jasik was a healer. He healed more quickly than the typical vampire and didn't require an instant refuel or rest. A few weeks ago, we had learned that I too was a healer, but when my temper got the best of me, and I showed another vampire ability, I accidentally unleashed my shield and used it against him. That was when he started to change. That was when his concern over what he'd done wrong when he changed me began to consume him.

I smiled at him. "I was just wondering about the other Hunters. Have I met them?"

"No. They're from covens on the east coast."

Oh.

"But they know of you and should be welcoming. They know of our task."

I see.

"Don't fret, my love," he said with a warm smile. Even without being a reader, Jasik could still understand the furrows and frowns, the smiles and laughs. He didn't need to be a reader to know what was playing in my head. I just wished he realized that himself.

We walked hand in hand toward the stairs that led to the first level—and, ultimately, to the dining hall. My stomach grumbled, even though I had fed from Jasik the night before.

"I wanted to talk to you about something," I said, uneasy.

He arched an eyebrow at me but didn't speak.

"I know you wanted to go east, but I think we should first travel south."

"To your old coven?"

I swallowed the lump in my throat. Jasik was cautious of my old coven because I still had lingering feelings for them. I didn't want him to over-think my request. "Yes. There is a powerful locater spell that we can do if we have their help. Sebastian and I can surely find her with it. It'll save time."

"But will they be willing to assist you?"

I frowned. "No, they won't, but I'll make them. They're bound to their beliefs and blinded by their fear, but I *am* family. Or, at least, I was. What's the worst that could happen? We'll argue, they'll see my stubbornness has only gotten worse in death, and they'll realize they have no choice."

He said nothing as we entered the dining hall, where the remaining members of our coven sat, thirstily drinking from jugs of blood. The floor to ceiling windows had the room bathing in moonlight, and just beyond the boulders, I heard the faint sound of waves crashing against the cliff. We walked to a corner table and sat beside Malik, Lillie, Jeremiah, and Sebastian.

"We've just been watching your boy, Avah," Lillie said, eying Sebastian.

"He most definitely is not *my* boy," I said. I refused to meet his gaze, but I could practically feel his cheeky grin form. I rolled my eyes.

Jasik gave me a curious look, probably trying to determine if I'd finally taken his side on the whole Sebastian situation. I squeezed his hand in response and give him a small smile. I didn't want him to know about the move Sebastian had made on me the night before. Jasik would have his head if he found out.

A vampire kitchen worker brought us mugs of blood, and we quickly slurped it down. We drank a second round and then a third. I didn't remember ever being this hungry. I assumed it was nerves.

"There will be a slight change of plans," Jasik said, and the Hunters glanced at him with curious eyes. Jasik turned to me.

Right. "We're going south first. Stopping by my old coven to attempt a locater spell with them and Sebastian. It won't take long—"

Pfft! Sebastian's lips rolled effortlessly in a rumble. I pursed my lips at him in anger, finally meeting his eyes.

"Do you have something to add, Sebastian? Because I believe we've already made it perfectly clear that you're coming *and* helping," I said.

"As a matter of fact, I do have something to add, Avah. No go."

"No go?" I asked.

"No go," he repeated.

No go! Sebastian was infuriating.

"I don't *do* witches," he added.

I gawked, appalled. What did that even mean? "Well, since you're half witch—"

"Ugh," he groaned. "Bugger off. That's a pathetic excuse."

"Tell me, then. Do you have a better idea?" I gave him a challenging glare. Of course he didn't have a better idea.

I ignored the wide, cheeky grin on Jeremiah's face as he watched us banter.

"Yes, we do it ourselves."

Seriously?

"It'll be more powerful if we have an entire coven behind it, Sebastian; you *should* know this," I said.

Now it was his turn to gawk, and I smiled in satisfaction.

"What have you to add?" Jasik cut in.

"What have I to add? *What have I to add?* What *don't* I have to add? Have you forgotten that I'm the only one you know who can help you, Avah?" I'd never seen Sebastian so upset. Gone was the playful lady killer.

"Why are you so upset about this? It won't even take that long," I said, shocked by his reaction to my plan.

He exhaled sharply and raised his pointer finger to me. His knuckles were white. The mug in his other hand shattered below his grip. Anger flared through me. How *dare* he treat me like this—in front of my own coven! I was sure we had onlookers, and I cringed at the thought.

"Sebastian, remove that finger before I bite it off," I said sternly as my fangs lowered.

We sat there, with his finger in my face and my fangs only a quick snatch away. I was only *slightly* curious to see if he could heal from this wound.

He retracted his finger and inhaled deeply, closing his eyes in what I assumed to be an attempt to control his temper. He opened his eyes again.

"Let me explain something to you, Avah. We have the best of both worlds, sure. I'm ecstatic to be what we are instead of like them," he said, flicking his head toward the other vampires and Hunters, "but I don't *do* witches anymore. I don't work with them. I don't associate with them. And if you were smart, you wouldn't, either."

I didn't know what to say.

"Witches are almost—*almost*—as bad as Rogues. At least with

Rogues, you know what you're getting. Witches have more brains. They're clever. They get you when you never even knew to be expecting it. Betrayal like that, it's the worst. I don't *do* witches."

"Repeating that a hundred times isn't going to make me understand any better. So, you don't *do* witches. Well, neither do I. Not since they cast me out. But I'm smart enough to know that we need their help to find Amicia. Be the bigger man, Sebastian. Step up."

He barked out a hard, insincere laugh. "This has nothing to do with being the bigger person, Avah. They're… them… those fucking witches," he stuttered, "can all burn in hell!" He pushed his chair back and stomped out of the dining hall.

"Well, that was interesting," Jeremiah said with wide eyes as he took a sip of blood. "I mean, dramatic much?" He stifled a laugh. I ignored the overwhelming sensation to slap him across the back of his head.

"Sebastian!" I called as I ran after him. The front door of the manor hung open, and vampires of the house stared into the empty abyss. I shook my head and followed him outdoors. I didn't have time to deal with his temper-tantrums.

"Leave me be," he said when I'd reached the front porch. He was sitting on the railing, his legs dangling in the air below him.

Realizing just how upset he truly was, I softened my approach.

"Sebastian," I said, resting a hand atop his shoulder. He recoiled, and I quickly removed my hand. I exhaled loudly.

"You don't understand, Avah," he said quietly.

"Isn't it your job to teach me?" I said with a small smile, waving away the Hunters who followed us onto the porch. They remained motionless—not moving closer but not leaving us be, either. I shook my head in frustration. How was I to deal with childish outbursts with onlookers?

"They can't be trusted."

"I know," I said honestly. I knew that the moment I'd turned and was shunned.

"No, you don't."

"Enlighten me, then."

He faced me, eyes hard. "I just—I don't know how much to tell you and how soon I should say it. What I know, it'll change your life forever, Avah." He shifted toward me. Well, that was progress.

"I think there's no better time than the present. We're leaving in less than an hour, and we need their help."

He grunted. "There's that word again: *need*. You speak so highly of them—even after all this." He waved his arms around, emphasizing the house, the vampires, everything my life had become.

"Well, we do need them… to find her." I crossed my arms

over my chest.

"You know what's so funny about those witches of yours?" he asked, swinging his legs over the rail and standing on the porch. His eyes burned into mine, turning into a fiery violet. I swallowed down the breath that had caught in my throat. He was close—too close. I felt his hot breath against my skin. I uncoiled my arms, fearing a fight.

I shook my head, unsure of what to say.

"They've never told you a single truth. That ritual? The incantations? *That's* what gave you The Power, not some god. Your coven chose you, not them," he said as he pointed to the sky. "They amplified the power that was already within you. Nothing else. Nothing more."

"That's not possible," I said. I shook my head in disbelief. My coven wouldn't betray me like that. My *mother* wouldn't betray me like that.

"Avah, *think* about it. There's more than one. You're looking at number two this very second. You still possess your witch magic. Be realistic. When you turned, that amplified power was still within you. *That's* why you're part witch, part vampire."

No! My world came crashing down as I recounted my childhood memories. Spirit users were chosen because we already had the ability to control the elements—just not quite like this.

Other affinities couldn't possess the ability to control the other elements, which is why there were never prophecies describing a fire witch as the chosen one. It wasn't in their nature. I couldn't deny that it made sense.

"It can't be," I whispered.

"Perk up, buttercup, because it is. The elders, the high priestesses, they knew what they were setting you up for. They knew others existed—most dead, others immortal."

"They couldn't have known. They wouldn't have done this to me." I began backing away. If *they* had chosen to do this to me, then *they*—my own coven, my own family—had intentionally set me up to die. No witch was born with this much power, because it completely consumed us. It wasn't natural. The body began to expel it almost as soon as it entered you. That was why so many had died after being *chosen*.

"You can't possibly believe they didn't know that the only others who existed were forced to turn in order to survive. Seriously, Avah. *Think* about it! I bet you were the only spirit user in your coven—or at least the only one they could play off as *chosen*." He used air quotes to emphasize his point. "After you've been around a while, you'll start to dig for information. Let me save you some time: witches invented this power scheme to wipe out an immortal species. And it's damned near working, too."

I was still backing away as he spoke, and I bumped into Jasik, who wrapped his arms around me, pulling my body against him. His eyes betrayed his pain. Did he know? Did they all know? I looked from one Hunter to the next. They remained cool, focused. Who could I trust? My new world of possibilities began to slowly crumble.

"Please tell me you didn't know," I said, speaking just above a whisper as I stared at Jasik's telling eyes. He shook his head, and I felt relieved. Of course they didn't know. Hunters were trained to take orders without questions. The thought to ask probably never occurred to him. But... did Amicia know?

"This doesn't make sense," I said. "I mean," I rubbed a hand through my hair, "it does, kind of, make sense, but it can't. It can't be true. How could they get away with this? They're sending their young to be slaughtered!"

"Because no one thinks to say, 'Hey, are you really a sociopathic homicidal maniac intent on annihilating an entire species simply because you don't understand them?' But think of all the time this would have saved if someone had my smart mouth," Sebastian replied. Though his words reeked with sarcasm, his tone didn't. He meant every word.

In an instant, my fear and pain had vanished, replaced by something more primal.

"We're going," I said, shrugging off Jasik's arms. "We're going to see them. Tonight."

I stormed back into the house and into the basement training quarters. I needed the truth. I needed to hear my mother tell me that she had lied to me my entire life, that she had knowingly and willingly *infected* me with a power that she *knew* would rip me apart from the inside out just so I could kill a few more vampires. Instead of trusting us to naturally get the job done, someone decided to sacrifice the youth for the greater good. Well, they sacrificed the wrong witch.

CHAPTER
FOUR

My mouth was in a hard line as I stared at myself in the floor-to-ceiling mirrors in the training room. My dark-brown hair looked eerily black beside my paling skin. I had always had a natural tan as a mortal, but the lack of sunlight slowly began to change that. To hunt for Amicia, I opted for the same outfit Jasik bestowed upon me mere weeks ago: black spandex shorts, black sports bra, and black shoes.

I closed my eyes, recalling my first encounter with the training quarters. Jasik had insisted I dress in these ridiculous garments. They helped to identify me as a Hunter, but also, they bared skin. This was a double benefit for those who fought against Rogues. They worked as a tease, forcing Rogues to think of nothing but blood, leaving them vulnerable in the attack. Besides ensuring

Rogues couldn't think straight, the clothes also allowed the Hunters to move freely, to focus on how their new forms moved. At the time, I hated the thought, but now, the unease within me subsided. Going practically sky-clad wasn't a foreseeable option at that time, but now it was my first choice.

I barely recognized the girl who stood before me. The thought was unnerving, but I shook the feeling quickly. I had to accept the inevitable: I couldn't face the witches *and* be the same girl they once knew. I needed to be a different person. I needed to suppress the innocence, the love, the longing. I needed to be the monster they created.

The other Hunters readied themselves around me but wisely chose to ignore my presence. Lillie's attire matched mine, though we looked nothing alike. My form was tall and curvy. Hers was short and thin. The spandex material fit my muscles snugly, where hers left room for gorging. The remaining Hunters wore only black shorts that cut off at their knees. Their exposed torsos were thick with muscles. Their look was oddly arousing and terrifying at the same time.

"Sebastian, you need to be armed," Jasik said, frustrated.

I watched them in the mirror. Jasik was nearly a foot taller than my five-foot-seven frame, and though Sebastian was tall, too, Jasik towered over him now. The few inches in height Jasik had on him seemed to lengthen when he took his leadership role seriously.

Sebastian arched an eyebrow. "Like I'd need shitty clothes or weapons to protect myself, mate." With his Australian accent playfully coating his words, it was hard to take his upset seriously.

"Yo, just wear the knife," Jeremiah said, placing the handle of a blade in Sebastian's hand. He then proceeded to individually curl each of Sebastian's fingers until he grasped the knife. "See, man. Not so bad." He flashed his swoon-worthy smile and turned to leave. Catching my eye, he gave me a quick wink. I blushed. The Hunters may not have enjoyed having Sebastian around, but I could always count on Jeremiah to lighten the mood.

Sebastian grumbled incoherently but slid the knife in his back pocket. "Happy?" he said to no one in particular.

His eyes lingered on me. I swallowed hard and faced the others. "Jasik?"

His eyes met mine, and I gestured toward the cabinet for my scabbard. It was thin and black; the material matched the crisscrossed back of my sports bra perfectly. I turned around so Jasik could slip it through my arms. It fit tightly against my frame and blended into my top. Next, Jasik handed me his treasured Celtic seax. It had been his father's, and Jasik graciously passed it down to me when he saw me eying it during our first training session. The two-foot-long blade had a slightly curved tip and a black handle with swirling silver lines that seemed to glitter. The handle also housed hematite, a powerful stone said to guide warriors in battle. It seemed fitting. Finally, I sheathed a dagger on my hip and faced the Hunters.

"Ready?" I asked. Muffled footsteps sounded overhead, and I glanced at the ceiling.

"More than you know," Malik replied. His eagerness to retrieve his priestess was top priority.

"Seems our visitors have arrived," Jasik said.

We tramped up the basement steps and to the front door, where the newcomers stood stoically, awaiting instructions. The four vampires before me had piercing neon eyes, ones that danced up and down my frame, taking in my presence. Their glowing eyes, a sign that magic ran freely through their blood, gave them away: they were the other Hunters. I nodded, and they didn't hesitate to return the gesture. They responded in unison, as if they'd been rehearsing.

"Thank you for coming on such short notice. I trust your travels went well," Jasik said, shaking each hand. "Help yourself to the house. We'll return as soon as we can."

The others followed Jasik's lead while Sebastian waited on the front porch. I knew he wasn't a social butterfly, but his behavior was blatantly disrespectful. I wanted to trust him—and to have him stay with us for the long haul—but even if he won me over, he'd need to make friends with the others, too. In an attempt to refute the possibly irreversible damage Sebastian caused, I offered my hand to each. The first two were women, who looked unmistakably similar. I was sure they were related somehow, but I didn't bother with questions. They didn't seem to be talkers— at least, they didn't seem to want to talk to *me*. After all, only we were privy to Sebastian's hybrid theories. To them, I was still an unknown. The final two were men, who took my hand in a vise-like grip. If I was but a mere mortal, the tiny bones in my hand surely would have shattered. I squeezed back and found comfort in their widening eyes and obvious winces. I gave them each a small smile and shrugged, like I couldn't help my strength.

And with that brief—and incredibly one-sided—encounter, the Hunters and I left the manor, escaping into the night.

"Relax, love," Jasik said, meeting my stride as the others followed in our wake.

Lillie couldn't keep her eyes off Sebastian. She had a serious trust issue. Briefly, I thought back to our first interaction. I had learned that she wanted a relationship with Jasik, but he never returned her feelings. When he met me, his attraction was instantaneous, and this infuriated her. Though, I couldn't blame her. I tried to put myself in her shoes. I'd be just as pissed. She was slowly opening up to me, so I didn't want to make a mistake by lecturing her on giving Sebastian a chance. Though, I wasn't sure if the mistake would be saying it and risking a possible friendship with her or saying it and then leaving Sebastian without a sitter. Both made me cringe. So I kept my mouth shut and eyes front.

"I'm fine," I said when I realized Jasik was waiting for an answer.

I focused on the surrounding woods. Darkness engulfed our world, and the creatures of the night had since come out to play. We were surrounded by trees that seemed to be as tall as skyscrapers in New York City. The lingering scent of salt water in the air tickled my senses.

"Surely what Sebastian explained isn't the truth. We'd have heard of it." He sounded confident.

"I'm not so sure, Jasik."

"Why do you doubt them?"

"Because I grew up with them." His question took me off-guard, but I answered without hesitation.

My mind wandered to the daily lectures I had received from the elder witches of my coven. I hadn't realized how much they despised vampires, but more importantly, I hadn't realized how much their bias affected me and *my* choices. I lived to kill vampires. I actually believed it was all I was truly good at. I completed my studies quickly so I could go on hunts. I lived for it, because I believed I was doing the right thing, keeping my coven safe. In reality, I was simply providing a service they needed. Nothing more. Nothing less.

"Just leave it be, Jasik," Lillie said from behind. She gave me a knowing sideways glance.

I gave her a grateful smile. I didn't often appreciate her using her gift as a reader to invade my personal thoughts, but tonight, I welcomed it. I needed to stay strong, to stay angry. It was the only way I'd actually say what needed to be said when we arrived.

Quickening my pace, I began running south, toward northern California, where my former witch coven resided, near the remote mountains of Shasta. I closed my eyes, relying on my heightened senses to guide me through the forest, and they did not disappoint. I wasn't sure how much time had passed when I reopened them again, but it was long enough to clear my mind and put on my game face.

"We're almost there," I said, slowing down, inhaling deeply. The smell of sage was strong here. It threw me off. We weren't close enough to the living quarters, where sage wafted through the air as part of protection spells. I stopped abruptly. Something was different.

I heard the faintest of noises: a slow, steady beat. It grew increasingly louder until it was pounding in my ears.

"Stop!" I said quickly, and the Hunters obeyed, though Jeremiah took a few more steps before turning to face me. We stood in a line, with Jeremiah in front of us.

"What—" he began before he was engulfed in flames.

His screams were piercing, invading all my senses. I sprang into action. I called upon air, quickly extinguishing the fire. Jasik fell to his knees, ripping into his wrist and mixing his blood into Jeremiah's wounds, expediting the healing process. The witches, members from my former coven, stepped from behind the thick pine trees, exposing themselves to us with an arrogant confidence. My cousins, Nina and Everly, stood with them. Everly threw her arms out before her, calling up fire again, and aimed it at me. Shocked, I stood motionless. She was trying to kill me. Her own flesh and blood cousin.

In an instant, Sebastian was beside me. He threw out his arm and called upon his affinities. His power drenched Everly and the surrounding witches in a tidal wave of water just before he knocked them off their feet with a blast of air. They were shivering in the brisk January air, stumbling to their feet. Sebastian's shield encompassed us. Tearing his angry gaze from the witches before us, he met my eyes.

"Did you expect a welcoming return?" he spat. He was still

angry—angry that he had to work with them, angry that I didn't believe him, angry that I'd turned him away.

"Well I certainly didn't expect to be fried by my own cousin!" I shouted, knowing they could hear me. I stalked toward Jeremiah, who was now standing with help from Jasik. His physical wounds were gone, but I was sure his pride was slightly tarnished.

"You good?" I asked, sincere.

"Yeah, I'm good. Gonna take a lot more than that," he said, staring at the witches.

"Good. Now," I said, returning to the edge of Sebastian's shield, "what's this I hear about a scam involving The Power?"

One by one, jaws of elder witches fell open. My cousins glanced around, confused.

"I've got all night. Do you?" I asked, confidently.

"Well, technically, we have until dawn," Malik whispered.

Sebastian gave me a curious eye. No, I didn't tell him. Keep your mouth shut.

"Or, you know, I could just blab my mouth around. I'm sure there are *plenty* of soon-to-be chosen ones out there who'd find the information I now have interesting."

"You need to leave," a voice called from behind. A haze surrounded her. She was a fire user attempting to keep warm.

"Did you really think I'd never discover the truth?" I asked, annoyed. "I have an eternity now!"

"Leave now or—"

"Or what? You'll attempt another pathetic attack? You're outnumbered and out-strengthed. Give it up. We're not here to hurt you, but we will protect ourselves," I threatened.

My cousins gasped. Seriously? You *just* tried to kill me. Did you not expect retaliation? Idiots.

"Get my mother," I ordered.

"She's not in charge anymore." My mother's earlier words echoed in my mind. I had begged for help when the Rogues were coming, and she had refused me. I was hurt more than anything, but she had warned me about *others* who were newly in charge of the coven since my transformation. I had brushed her words away as nothing but excuses.

"Get my mother, or you're next," I said slowly, confidently. My fangs lengthened, and I released a low growl. I was sure my violet irises were burning against the blackness of the night. I hoped I was intimidating.

The woman laughed. "You don't remember me, do you, Avah Taylor?"

I held my stance. She was right. I didn't know who she was, but more importantly, I didn't care. She *would* help us.

"You were such a powerful girl, even as a child. We had high hopes for you."

We? Who was this woman?

"Though, now that I think of it, it doesn't surprise me that your memory has failed you. It's been quite a long time, hasn't it?"

"Who are you?" I shuffled through my memory, trying to place her. She did look familiar, but nothing came to mind.

"Oh, silly me. I shall remind you. My name is Eloise Taylor."

Breath escaped me. "Grandma?" I said, my voice shaking. I hadn't seen my grandmother since my father had been murdered. It had been over twenty years.

"Yes, dear, and I've come to clean up your mother's mess."

I only remembered three things about my grandmother: she was a terrifying woman, she constantly took mysterious business trips, and she was one hell of a witch. She hated my mother, hated that my father married such a free-spirited woman. Growing up, I was sure she hated me, too. I never heard from her, and on the rare occasions she visited, she spoke only to my father. I learned to keep my eyes down and lips sealed when she was in the house.

"Can't say you've aged well," I spat. If my insult affected her, she didn't show it.

"Back to those ridiculous orders. Your mother is no longer in charge, and you would do well to keep whatever information you think you've become entitled to hushed. Word of mouth is fast growing, Avah, and I know where you reside. Leave now."

Sebastian barked out a hard laugh. The Hunters and I glanced cautiously at him. Was he at the brink? Had I pushed him too far by bringing him here? Had he finally lost his mind?

"Oh, bugger off! Lady," he said, stepping forward. "You may be one strong bitch, but I have power you've never dreamed of. It's taking everything within me to not pop your cherry all over these pathetically spelled woods in an effort to simply remove an increasingly annoying factor from my life. Instead, I'm going to ask you one time and one time only: will you *please* retrieve Avah's mother? And you can be damned sure the next time we speak about this, I will have lost all my manners."

He was fuming. I was sure the air actually sizzled as it touched his skin.

"Dude, did you *really* just talk about popping her cherry?" Jeremiah whispered as he shuddered.

Lillie took a sharp jab at his side with an elbow, and he winced, still weak from his near-death experience.

My grandmother didn't move, didn't speak. Her lips were in a hard line, and the *v* shape between her brows deepened. I was sure she was assessing her options. Take on four Hunters and two hybrids and risk wiping out her coven? Or bring my mom here? The choice seemed obvious.

"Step forward," she said.

Suddenly, my mother emerged from just past the trees, and my heart sank in response. Her eyes were swollen, her nose puffy. Her usually tanned skin was pink, raw. Her frame was frail, weak. The woman before me was nothing like the strong witch I'd grown up idolizing. No, this was the face of a battered woman, one who was struggling to survive.

"Hello, Avah," she said, her voice hoarse. A small smile slowly began to form across her lips, and my grandmother slapped her across the face. My mother's frail frame collapsed to the ground, and I jumped to her side, leaving the protection of the shield. I pulled her into my arms, resting her head against me as it lolled over. She was out cold. Jeez. Just how weak was she? I glanced up at the witches who towered over me and my mother as we slumped to the ground.

"What have you done to her?" I snarled.

"I haven't even begun to reprimand her for her actions, Ms. Taylor," my grandmother responded. "She has broken more laws than I can count!"

"I guess that doesn't speak highly of your counting skills now does it, lady?" Lillie interjected.

I was shocked she defended my mother, and in a moment of weakness, I turned to glance at her. My moment's distraction was all my grandmother needed. She pounced forward, with unusual grace for a woman of her age, and wrapped her fingers around my neck, calling upon fire.

CHAPTER
FIVE

I screamed as my blood began to boil. My skin, unable to contain the liquid heat, bubbled until it pockets burst. The needle-prick flames danced across every inch of my frame in constant, nagging thrusts. Images flashed before my eyes. Sebastian was before me, ripping my grandmother's hand from my neck. I collapsed onto someone from behind; arms enveloped me in a soothing embrace. When I broke free of her deadly, burning touch, the pain began to subside. I leaned against my protector, dazed. My blood quickly healed my fried brain. Jasik sat behind me, lifting me as I rested against his body. He offered his dripping wrist to me, and though I too was a healer and didn't need his offering, I craved it. I swallowed him down, the last bit of magic needed to heal me, and I licked my lips as I sat up, my mother still unconscious next to me. My hands instinctively brushed against my throat. Smooth skin greeted me.

With my strength rejuvenated, I was able to take in my surroundings. The witches around me were screaming; most had already fallen to my grandmother's side. And that's when I saw it. Her neck had been snapped, her body lay contorted, her head angled awkwardly. I tensed at the sight. Her legs were sprawled about. Two perfect puncture marks branded her neck, and her mouth was blotted in quickly drying blood.

I looked to Sebastian, the obvious culprit, who was licking his lips in disgust.

"I considered ripping her heart out but thought this would be much more satisfying. She'll awaken as the one being she can't stand to be near: a vampire. And then she'll be left to choose: to break her morals and take her own life or live her life as a creature she despises. Choices. Choices. It's almost too good to be true." Sebastian smirked.

My heart leapt. He saved me. Again. I felt nothing for the loss of the woman before me. She didn't deserve such respect.

Sebastian raised his fingers in a *tsk tsk* motion as my cousin began to call upon her element.

"No, no, no. No ending it for her. *She* needs to make the decision." I was surprised Everly was brave enough to burn her body. She had definitely gained more courage since I'd left. I glanced back down at my mom's frail frame.

"Mom?" I said, rubbing her hair from her eyes. I looked up at Jasik, and he gave me a small smile. The remaining Hunters watched the witches closely. Sebastian's shield had been lowered, and we were all exposed. I thanked the heavens that Malik, Lillie, and Jeremiah had the sense to keep watch, because I sure didn't.

"Okay," Sebastian said, clapping his hands together and rubbing them quickly. "Who do I have to eat around here to get a decent locater spell concocted?"

I rolled my eyes. Seriously?

"Relax," I said, as the witches began to slowly back away, finally choosing their own lives over the dead woman at their feet. "I meant what I said. We aren't—well, we *weren't*—going to hurt you. Sebastian's right. We just need a quick locater spell done, and we'll be on our way, leaving you to, you know, clean up all this." I looked at my dead grandmother lying at my feet.

"Everyone calm down," a voice said, and I faced my aunt. "We'll do the spell, but then you need to leave." I supposed she would be in charge now that my mom and grandmother were indisposed.

"Great," I said, standing. I pulled my mom into my arms. "Let's get you ready." I spoke softly as I teetered back so my mom's head rested against my shoulder.

The witches opened like the Red Sea as I walked past them. They watched me with wide eyes. Surely, it was odd for them to see a creature like me show an emotion they thought we couldn't feel. I still cared for my mother—even though she was part of the reason I was in this mess. I buried the thought for another time and entered my former home. Taking my mother into our ritual preparation room, I set her down gently on the floor. I filled the tub with hot water and turned to face the Hunters, who had followed me into the house.

"We can't separate, Avah." Jasik's voice was stern. I knew there was no room to argue.

"Wait outside the door," I said.

The Hunters did as they were told, but Jasik lingered.

"Jasik, I need to bathe her, get her cleaned up. You need to go. I'll be fine."

"I know. It's just—I'm sorry. I'm sorry this has happened to her." His face seemed sunken as if he were flashing to an unwelcome memory from his own past.

I smiled to reassure him, and he left us in peace.

With the door closed, I faced the tub again and spelled the water. It would remain warm for her. I added tea leaves and lavender to help speed her healing process, assuming she wouldn't take my blood if I

DANIELLE ROSE

offered it to her. With her bath set, I disrobed her and carefully lowered her into the tub. I rested her head against the back of the tub and scooped water into a nearby cup, slowly running it through her hair. Water splashed on the floor, but I didn't care. Cleaning the ritual spaces were no longer my concern.

"Mother, what have you done? How'd we get into this mess?" I asked as I began massaging shampoo into her dingy hair. I let the soap lather and bubble under my hands as I focused on her low, shallow breaths. As much as I hated what she had done to me, she was still my mother. I couldn't bear seeing her this way.

"What did they do to you?" I whispered, tears threatening to spill. It never occurred to me that my mom would be punished for my choices. I exhaled quickly, once again pushing my emotions down.

I rinsed her hair and squeezed conditioner into the palm of my hand. As I worked her hair clean and soft, I talked to her. I explained my new life and how it wasn't as bad as I thought it was going to be. I told her about Jasik and my feelings for him. I noted that I wasn't so sure about Sebastian, but I wanted to know him, to trust him.

"Sebastian can really help me, Mom. He knows so much about this world. I thought I did, too, but then I realized I don't really know anything except the lies you told me."

I shook my head as anger worked its way back into my mind.

I rinsed her hair free of conditioner and wrapped it in a thick towel so she wouldn't get the chills. I couldn't find body soap, so I lathered her skin with shampoo.

"You know what's crazy? I almost died today. *Grandma* almost killed me. Everly *threatened* to kill me, and my own aunt told me to never return…" I exhaled deeply, wincing as my fingers passed over a rib that protruded after healing awkwardly. "Just another day, I guess. How messed up is my life? Seriously." I shook my head. "Doesn't even faze me." I splashed the water around to rinse her soapy skin.

"I wish I could talk to you, Mom," I said as I grabbed her bony hand. I placed a soft kiss to each thin finger. "Please tell me you didn't know about this. Please tell me you didn't do this to me." I whispered as I spoke, but not because lingering vampires could eavesdrop. I whispered because I was growing tired. I was tired of believing in the witches. Tired of protecting and defending their honor. Tired of the stories. I just wanted peace.

I was sure I'd sooner get an eternity of violence before a lifetime of happiness.

Slowly, her eyes began to flutter.

"Mom? It's Avah. Can you hear me?" My voice squeaked, and I cleared my throat.

"Avah," she whispered.

"Yes, Mom. It's me. Can you open your eyes?"

Her eyes fluttered again. She was weak, too weak.

Reluctantly, I bit into the palm of my hand and squeezed it shut before quickly pressing it against her lips. She drank. Before my eyes, she began to heal. Her sunken face fattened, her thin frame expanded until I could no longer see her bones. Her eyes shot open, and she pushed my hand away, spitting out the blood that coated her tongue. She hacked as she grasped the tub's edge. In dry heaves, she attempted to spill the contents of her stomach onto the floor, but it was no use. My blood had already worked its magic. It was part of her now, and she'd have to live with that betrayal until she stepped at death's door. Internally, I smiled.

"How could you?" she yelled, wiping crimson streaks from her mouth. She cupped bathwater between her hands and splashed her face, eliminating any trace of my gift to her.

"You were going to die, Mom," I said matter-of-factly. How could she be upset with me? *They* were torturing her!

"I was fine! I didn't need your help." She was lying. We both knew that. But she was too proud to admit it.

"Maybe you should direct your anger at the root of the problem instead of taking it out on me," I said as I stood from where I crouched beside her. I tossed the towel on the floor beside the tub. "Get out. We have work to do."

I turned so she could change in privacy. I crossed my arms and tapped my foot angrily as I stared out the small window that overlooked the backyard and ritual circle space. The small clearing of our yard was surrounded by the woods. Only weeks ago, I stood there, offering myself to the gods as a vessel used to harness The Power. I heard her approach me, but I refused to turn back. She had gone too far this time.

"Don't," I said as the wind shifted around me. In the window's reflection, I watched her hand still in the air, hovering just above my shoulder. "I don't need your anger or your pity." I was sure she had thought the same thing.

"Avah, I'm sorry. But please, don't do that again."

"So I should just let you die?"

Her teeth scraped together as she clenched her jaw, the noise deafening.

I turned to face her. "How could you?" I spoke barely above a whisper, and I wondered if she could even hear me.

"I had no choice, Avah. You were the only one fit to join the elite." She gave me the tone she used when she was issuing commands as a high priestess. I was raised to never question her orders when she gave this tone, but I didn't care anymore. I'd force her to explain herself even if it was the last thing she did.

"The elite? You mean the other *chosen ones*?" I hoped my

dramatic emphasis stung. She winced, and I was pleased.

"Yes."

"Well, I hate to break it to you, but they're *dead*. But then again, you should know that."

"They're not all dead, Avah. Well, not yet—"

"Seriously?" I gawked. "Did you really just use that as a defense?" Had she gone insane since I left, too?

"Avah, I did what needed to be done as the high priestess of this coven. I didn't tell you, because as a mere coven member, you weren't privy to that information." She used her no-nonsense mom voice this time. She probably thought I'd back down, because in the past, I had done just that.

"I think that since *my* life was being stolen from me by *you*, my *mother*, I should have been *privy* to that information, don't you?" I snarled.

"No. It would have made you weak. You needed to think clearly in battle."

"You mean during the few remaining battles I could fight before my insides were torn apart, and I succumbed to this poison within me?"

She exhaled quickly. "Don't be so dramatic, Avah. This is centuries in the works. Who was I to stop it? Who was I to not join the others who put our cause before anything else?"

"That's the problem, Mom! You should have put *me* first! I *needed* you! It was your job to protect me, not sacrifice me!" I couldn't stop the tears from flowing. They burned as they thrashed down my cheeks. She reached to wipe them away, and I smacked her hand back with enough force to make her lose her balance.

"It's in your best interest to keep your distance," I grumbled.

Her look of shock softened the anger within me. She'd never see it my way, and I'd never see it her way. I had said what I needed to, and now, I'd have to live with what she'd done to me. I decided to get to the point of my visit before my anger toppled over and couldn't be controlled.

"We need your coven's help." She gaped at me. Was it because I needed their help? Or was it because I'd finally refused to call them *my* coven? Did she really expect anything less? "My high priestess has been taken by Rogues. We need to find her." The words escaped me. I referred to Amicia as my high priestess in front of my former high priestess. I wondered if it hurt my mother to hear such a thing. Out of spite, I hoped it crippled her.

She nodded.

"Good. And when this is over, we're done."

"Avah—"

"No, don't you dare *Avah* me. You have no right to speak my name. I won't come for you. I won't think of you. I expect the same in return. And while you live your pathetic existence, I want you to remember that you witches are sacrificing the only people who would die to protect you. If you witches want a war, you got one."

I turned, storming toward the door and ripping it open. It smashed into the wall, falling to the ground in pieces. The Hunters stood, staring in disbelief. I was sure they'd heard our encounter; I wasn't exactly quiet.

"Don't start," I warned as I pushed past them. "I expect you at circle in five minutes, Tatiana." I had never called my mother by her first name. I hoped it would instill the pain and agony she had put me through. Her betrayal stung core deep.

As we entered the backyard ritual space, I stalked past the non-magical members of my former coven. They hurriedly attempted to escape us by closing themselves off within their homes. I ignored their curious glances toward me. I wasn't in the mood to show them I was the same girl they once knew. As far as I was concerned, they were *all* in on this ridiculous cover-up hoax.

My mother approached from behind, now dressed in her ritual cloak. Her attire matched that of the other witches, who already stood in their places for the ritual. My aunt waved her sage stick around my mother and let her pass into the circle. If she noticed my mother's suddenly healthy demeanor, she didn't mention it aloud.

"Ready for this?" I asked Sebastian as I turned to face him.

"Ready to get it over with."

"Me, too," I agreed. I was ready to walk away and never turn back.

"Let's stay positive," Malik said.

"I am. I positively want to get the fuck out of here," Sebastian answered, and I chuckled. If only he knew...

I grabbed Sebastian's hand, our fingers intertwining. I ignored Jasik as he tensed beside me at my show of affection. Sebastian smiled down at me, his violet eyes staring intensely into mine. His chin-length sandy-brown hair was pulled back into a tight ponytail.

"Let's go," I whispered.

In unison, we walked, hand in hand, toward the circle. My mother waved the sage stick around us, cleansing our auras. We turned, and she repeated the process. We turned to face her again.

"How do you enter?" she asked us. Her eyes were wet with tears, but I ignored them.

"In perfect love and perfect trust," we answered.

We entered the circle, the familiar pull of magic tugging within me. Sebastian's eyes burned brightly as he stared straight ahead. I wondered if he missed this. I was sure it had been

DANIELLE ROSE

hundreds of years since he last participated in a ritual.

Within the circle of witches, who now chanted in Latin, a spell to strengthen our power, their arms out beside them, palms up, and their heads tilted back, burned four blue candles. The candles represented the four corners and the element associated with each one.

Still hand in hand, Sebastian and I maneuvered through the lit candles and sat down, legs crisscrossed, facing each other.

Together, our fangs lengthened, and we bit into our wrists. Quickly, we slapped our wounds together, dripping wrist to dripping wrist. I inhaled quickly as his power seeped into me through the tiny puncture wounds. With a heaving chest and glossy eyes, he stared down at me. The air tingled around us, and our surroundings began to fade away as our blood magic took control.

I no longer heard the chanting witches. I no longer saw the pacing Hunters.

There was only me and Sebastian and the unfamiliar feeling of his essence coursing through my veins.

My skin was slick, and I ignored the overwhelming urge to reach up and wipe away the drip of blood slipping down Sebastian's muscular jaw.

"*Spiritum Spiritu voccat te. Spiritu Spiritus indicaret mihi,*" I whispered, calling to the spirit power within Sebastian and me, begging it to connect with Amicia's essence. *"Spiritum Spiritu voccat te. Spiritu Spiritus indicaret mihi."* This time, I spoke more forcefully.

The wind around us grew stronger, the air heating as Sebastian and I connected with Amicia. I closed my eyes.

"Sebastian," I whispered. "I'm connected."

My body swayed as I fought to stop myself from toppling over. Sebastian's hand reached out, steadying me.

I could see only images in flashes—all things Amicia had seen.

"I see a young girl. A village. Slaughtered. There are bodies everywhere. The girl's crying, her face in her hands. They're bloody." I didn't understand. I didn't see anything familiar. "Everything looks... old. Like it's from a different time."

"Keep focusing." Sebastian's calm voice echoed around me. "Move forward in the vision."

I nodded, my head too heavy. I fell over and into Sebastian's arms. My head rested against his chest. His heart was pounding against my ear. I couldn't hear anything but his breath and the steady, strong beat of his heart. I had to pull away, or I'd lose her.

Understanding my need, Sebastian pushed me back upright, and I sat on my own again. My arm ached where my hand grasped Sebastian's. I wanted to pull it back, but his power was my connection to Amicia. Our bleeding wrists must stay bound. My wound tingled as the magic within us attempted to heal it, but the ritual was meant to maintain vulnerability, and until we separated, we'd continue to bleed together.

"I see… Jasik. Malik. They're crouched, I think. Somewhere dark. They're weak, hungry. Sorting through trash. Cobblestone pathways and crumbling buildings everywhere. It's old. Everything is old." I was confused again. How was Amicia seeing the Hunters if they were here? Now.

"You're seeing her past," Sebastian answered. "Keep moving. You need to hurry." He sounded weak.

I gasped but quickly closed my mouth. "I see the battle. I see her. They have her." We didn't doubt my last statement, but I still needed to say it aloud. The Hunters were lingering just beyond our closed circle. They watched and listened as I explained what I was seeing.

"Good, keep going. You're almost there. Stay strong. Keep the connection alive." His voice was so soft I barely heard him. I knew he couldn't hold on much longer without refueling. Reaching Amicia took more power than we'd realized.

My eyes jolted open as I screamed. My wrist fell from Sebastian's, our connection broken. He toppled over, breathing heavily. In the corner of my eye, I saw Jasik dash toward us, but the witches stopped him by calling on air. He skidded backward, his heels never leaving the ground.

"Do not break this circle!" my aunt ordered.

Unable to hold my weight any longer, I fell to the ground beside Sebastian. I silently thanked him, hoping he was still strong enough to read my mind at that moment.

Sebastian? Did you see that? He gave me no response. I blinked away the images that would haunt my eternity.

Quickly, the witches closed the circle, and Jasik was before me, lifting me into his arms. My head rolled back, and I looked to Sebastian, who was being carried between Malik and Jeremiah. He slowly grinned his cunning sideways smile, but it held no power. It was weak, forced.

"I like doing magic with you," Sebastian whispered. The same odd sensation burned within me as I realized I liked doing magic with him, too.

I smiled at him. "It was an experience."

I blinked, and we were in the front yard. Jasik set me down beside Sebastian.

"They need to feed," he said. Jasik lowered his wrist to my mouth, and I sank my fangs into his skin. I ignored the looks of disgust on the faces of the witches around us. I glanced at Sebastian, who was already feeding from Lillie's wrist.

Interesting.

When we'd had our fill, we pulled away, visibly stronger.

"Tonight, we hunt," Jasik said, stroking my brow bone with his thumb.

I nodded and stood. I was still weak, the lingering effects of magic clouding my mind. Soon, it would be gone. The thought left me feeling... empty. I looked at my wrist. The marks were already gone. It was as if we'd never practiced the blood magic that would lead us to Amicia.

"Thanks for your help," I shouted over my shoulder as we slowly sauntered away, noticing that my grandmother's body had been moved. Briefly, I wondered where she was and if they truly would make her decision for her. I shook my head at the thought. I was a wash of emotions, but I couldn't let them control me.

As we began to leave the witches, and my old life, behind, everything was becoming clearer.

I turned on my heel and pulled at what little strength I had within me, and in an instant, I was before my aunt. "I may want nothing to do with any of you anymore, but if you hurt my mother because of what happened here today, I'll come back, and I'll rip your throat out and feed it to your newly turned daughters."

Ignoring her gaping eyes, I gave her my biggest Miss America smile—one I'd learned from Lillie—and stalked toward the

Hunters, refusing to meet my mother's eyes. I may have showed them the monster they wrongly assumed I was, but it was worth it. If they wanted to punish my mother, they had plenty of reasons to do so without blaming this visit on her.

I met Jasik's concerned look and smiled, hoping I was reassuring him. I was an emotional mess, but I didn't want him to use that against me. If what Amicia unknowingly showed me was true, then the Hunters needed me. They weren't strong enough to face what was to come alone.

"Tonight, we feed. Tomorrow, we find her."

CHAPTER SIX

We hunted in silence, hoping to not frighten potential food. I closed my eyes, focusing on the sounds of the night.

Snap!

My eyes shot open, and I dashed toward the noise. The trees at my sides blurred into one as I raced toward possible food. I came to a near-screeching halt, watching a herd of deer grazing before me—the perfect meal. There were five. My skin tingled as the air shifted. The Hunters now stood beside me, and in one leap, we revealed ourselves to the animals. We killed them quickly and drank furiously, draining everything they had. When finished, I couldn't help but feel sorrow. I had lived my mortal life beside animals, cherishing their existence, and now, I hunted them daily.

Running his tongue over his teeth, Jeremiah said, "So are we going to just avoid the massive elephant in the room or..."

I rolled my eyes, knowing he was referring to me.

"What did you see?" Jasik asked softly. His hand reached for mine and squeezed it lightly.

I remained silent. Should I tell them? I looked from Sebastian to Lillie. They were readers. Had they already read my mind?

Sebastian slowly shook his head, glancing from Lillie to me. What did that mean? Lillie couldn't read my thoughts? But clearly, Sebastian could. But he hadn't answered me earlier, after we'd practiced our blood magic. What did that mean? Could he not read my thoughts then? We were both weak, too weak. Did that affect his ability to invade my mind?

"It was cold. Very cold," I finally said.

"How do you know?" Lillie cut in. It was a fair question. As a vampire, cold didn't affect us, but I could feel the change in temperature. It was an odd sensation: to know I should be cold but was not.

"The air was crisp and clear. It held a tingly sensation. Steam clouds escaped lips. It was pretty obvious that it was freezing temperatures."

"What else?" Malik said, his tone clear.

They were antsy. They wanted to know if I had all the

85

information we needed to find her. I wiped my shaking hands against my bare legs in an attempt to hide my discomfort.

"She's close. I felt her nearness. I just don't know exactly where she is."

"Okay. So cold. Close. This is good, right? I mean, how many places could that be?" Jeremiah asked.

"I don't know," Jasik said, running a hand through his hair. "Northern Washington State? Borderline Canada?"

"I don't think they'd keep her *that* close," I said. "They'd want to get her farther away from us, right?" Our coven resided on national forest land. We were on the coast but so deep within the remote lands that no one even knew we were there. Our property was on the northern west coast of Washington State, so keeping Amicia *that* close to us wouldn't have been the Rogue's best plan to date. But they weren't known for being an intelligent bunch of people.

"Right. So Canada? Montana has potential. It's cold this time of year, very remote."

Sebastian visibly tensed, and I arched my eyebrow at him. What did he know?

"Maybe." Montana seemed like a good guess. I kept my eyes on Sebastian. *You know something…*

"So, basically, we know nothing," Lillie said with a stern

voice. *Well, not all of us.*

"Lillie." Jasik's tone was harsh, abrupt. It snapped me out of my trance, and I finally tore my eyes from Sebastian's unyielding gaze.

"No, she's right. I screwed up the ritual." I wiped the dew from my forehead.

"What else did you see?" Malik asked, probing.

I swallowed. "I saw them torturing her. I felt her terror. I don't... I don't even know if she's still alive." I spoke quietly, unable to meet the Hunters' eyes.

"We need to move quickly, Jasik," Malik said.

"The sun will rise soon, too. We need to find shelter."

I glanced at Sebastian but quickly looked away. Was now the time to tell them about my nifty new power? How much information could they handle in one day? I shook my head in frustration. I knew so much, yet also so little.

"There's—there's something else." I swallowed down the air that threatened to choke me.

They didn't speak.

"In my vision, there were at least a dozen sets of red irises on me as I looked through her eyes. They took turns torturing and feeding from her."

Lillie gasped.

"But then it spanned out, the vision. Like an aerial view or something. That's when I lost it, the connection." I shuddered as I replayed what I saw.

"What did you see?" Jasik asked, his eyes concerned.

"I saw… more." I kicked the hard-packed ground at my feet.

"More?" Jasik asked.

I nodded and sat. I played mindlessly with broken twigs and frozen grass.

"More what?" Jeremiah asked.

"Of them," I said breathlessly.

"Avah, how many did you see?" Jasik spoke the words slowly, carefully, as if he too was afraid of my answer.

"Hundreds. I can't be sure. But I'd call it an army." I couldn't believe the words even as I spoke them.

"An army? Of Rogues?" Malik swallowed hard, his jaw clenching. I had never seen him fearful. It was uncomfortable to see him weakened.

It seemed as though an eternity passed before someone finally spoke again.

"We need help," Jasik said.

Sebastian huffed. "Obviously, but there aren't enough Hunters for this kind of army."

"What do you suggest?" Jasik responded, annoyed. I could tell he had had enough of Sebastian's negativity. I pulled my legs toward me and rocked slowly.

Please, Sebastian. Help us. He could pretend to have no access to my thoughts, but I knew better. Sebastian had already admitted that we had access to all Hunter abilities. I just needed to learn to tap into them. Sebastian had centuries to perfect this. He needed to stop playing games with me.

"I have some connections. In Montana," Sebastian finally said.

Hmm. Montana? Interesting. I stood and crossed my arms.

"As do we," Jasik responded.

"Not this kind of connection," Sebastian replied, glancing at me.

I gasped. *More.*

I nodded. "I want to meet them." An odd mix of emotions overwhelmed me: I was giddy at the chance to meet more hybrids, but I was also worried. What would they be like? How has The Power affected them? Staring at them would be like looking in a mirror...

"Well, pet. Today's your lucky day. They'll welcome you, but them," he said, glancing at the Hunters, "not so much."

"Why? They're Hunters, too."

"Whoa. Wait a sec. Are we talkin' more hybrids?" Jeremiah asked, eyes gaping.

"You don't miss a thing, do you?" Sebastian asked.

I groaned. "Not this again. Can't we all just get along? For Amicia?"

"For Amicia?" Sebastian snorted. "I have no connection to her."

Malik stepped forward, as if he had concluded to correct this situation immediately. I placed my hand on his arm, and he tensed beneath it. His eyes met mine, and I silently begged him to let me handle this. He released a long breath and stepped back.

"You have a connection to me, Sebastian, and I am asking you—no, *begging* you—to stop this, to help us, to help me." I pleaded with my eyes.

He shook his head. "Fine, but when this is done, I'm gone. I'm a bit tired of this lacking hospitality."

Seriously? Have you not heard that 'you get what you give' saying?

He rolled his eyes, and I smiled. I knew he could hear my thoughts.

"So what now?" Lillie asked. I had almost forgotten about her. She hadn't spoken since I confided my vision in them.

"How many hybrids are there?" I asked. Hopefully enough to take down the Rogues awaiting us.

"Not enough to stop this army, but enough to make a difference."

"Good," I said, nodding. "Let's go, then."

Sebastian gave me his killer smile and turned on his heel.

"Keep up. Time to chase the night," he said with a wink.

The sun! How could I have forgotten the sun? I looked east, where the sun was already beginning to slowly rise. My blood boiled at the thought.

My feet pounded against the ground as I attempted to keep up with Sebastian's long, strong strides. To an onlooker, we were but a blur. I was sure humans had seen vampires before. In that moment when they thought they'd seen something and had to blink twice or did a double take, they probably spotted one. But in a split second, we were gone, and their minds' rationalization sunk in. They never knew they were but feet away from what stood at the top of the food chain.

We were quickly over the eastern mountains of the state and entered the flatland zone. Flatlands weren't friends to creatures of the night, and I quickly glanced at the Hunters beside me. Sweat beaded on their foreheads as they strained to keep up, to keep alive. I returned my gaze to Sebastian, who seemed humored by the occasion.

"Keep up," he yelled. "We're going to Daniels County."

"Let me guess," I yelled back. "That's the farthest county in the state?"

"Pretty much," he chuckled.

I groaned. Of course.

I gasped as I slowly watched the sun's rays shine brightly against the ground. A line separated what remained of the night and what was becoming the day. The sun quickly dominated, eliminating any trace of our safety. I swallowed. This was it. I whipped my head from side to side. There was no escape. The trees that surrounded us would provide little shelter for the Hunters.

"Here!" Sebastian yelled, breaking my thoughts, and he leaped forward before falling back to the ground. He slid into the shallow hole of a hidden cave's entrance. I hadn't even noticed it. It was small and low to the ground, clearly hidden from passersby. I was sure Lillie and I could fit through easily, but the others? The hole was probably half the size of their width. I imagined them attempting to squeeze through as the sun's rays hit their exposed skin.

I sent up a silent prayer to whatever god or goddess was listening, and I mimicked his move, slipping into the cave. The ground disappeared as I entered, and I was free-falling. I threw my hands up, trying to grab onto something, anything to break my fall. There was nothing. Nothing but darkness and the stench of death. I wondered how many thought exploring the cave would be a fun adventure and then died here after the initial leap.

Whoosh!

I closed my eyes as I was enveloped by a foreign substance. It embraced me completely, and I was tightly bound. I inhaled quickly, the substance stealing my breath away. I choked it out, unable to breathe, to see, to concentrate.

Whoosh! Whoosh! Whoosh!

I vaguely heard the others join the abyss beside me.

Focus! Breathing was an unbreakable habit of a mortal lifetime. My immortal existence didn't require breath the way my mortal one did. I spit the substance out and stopped myself from involuntarily sucking it back in. My heaving chest burned. The substance tingled against my un-working lungs.

I shrieked as I smacked against rock, and my legs snapped.

I reached down aimlessly, but I could already feel the bones reforming. I pushed my arms around, searching for safety, for a way to be released. A hand clenched mine and pulled me to safety. I opened my eyes and found I was held in Sebastian's arms, the substance still dripping down my face. Closing my eyes again, I sucked in air and choked out the remaining bits that threatened to suffocate me.

"Shhh," he soothed. "You're fine."

"What was that?" I choked out, my fingers digging into his shoulders.

He smiled. "Water." I opened my eyes, blinking. Water?

I gaped at him and looked around. We sat in an iridescent pool of murky water. I unhinged from Sebastian. The water was deep; my legs swished back and forth as I struggled to stay upright.

"First time swimming since you've changed?" Sebastian asked.

I nodded. "It's wasn't exactly the experience I remembered." I blushed, embarrassed. I had completely overreacted.

"Not quite." He smiled at me, tucking loose strands of my hair behind my ear.

Suddenly, I was acutely aware of his proximity. He was close to me as I swayed in the water. His body was firm, arousing. I pushed myself away and swam to the edge.

Jasik offered his hand, and I grasped it. He pulled me up, rubbing his hand against my back.

"Are you okay?" he asked.

I nodded.

He smiled and placed a kiss on my forehead.

"It was different, wasn't it?"

"Very. I thought I was going to die." I laughed. Only I could make vampirism this dramatic.

"Very few things will end your life, Avah. Water isn't anywhere on that list." He winked and released me.

Stepping back, I took in our surroundings.

The entrance to the cave was fifty or so feet above us and provided enough light for my heightened senses to explore. The air was dank and held a formidable staleness. I found myself frowning at the scent as I chomped my jaws open and closed. The scent lingered, coating my tongue. I ran my tongue against my teeth and spat. The walls were covered in slick dew, and I couldn't help but scrunch my nose at the sight.

"This way," Sebastian said as he lifted himself from the dark water. He pointed toward a small tunnel.

"Where does that lead?" I asked.

"Headquarters."

I gaped at him. Headquarters? Just how advanced were these people?

He barked out a hard laugh. "I'm kidding. You should see your face."

I rolled my eyes. "I should see a *shower*." I ran a hand across my skin and shivered. I could still feel the murky, dirty water on me. It clung lifelessly to my pores as it pried, attempting to seep into every part of my being. I was fairly sure I'd never go swimming again. Ever.

"The tunnel leads us out of here. Seems to be our only option."

We took to foot, squeezing down the narrow hallways. I glanced back at the Hunters. They crouched as they maneuvered through. Lillie and I were the only ones short enough to semi-comfortably walk without scraping against the walls. The tunnel seemed endless, and I silently thanked the gods and goddesses that I wasn't claustrophobic.

The tunnel opened to a wide room that nearly mirrored the previous room, sans the exits and waterhole. It was a large, circular, candle-lit dungeon of no escape. And in its center, several dozen sets of violet irises stared back at me.

CHAPTER
SEVEN

I swallowed hard as their eyes lingered on my frame. I was sure my newborness was obvious to the new onlookers.

"Hello, Sebastian," a voice said. The woman was sitting, sharpening her knife between two rocks. She focused solely on her work, never gracing us with a glance. "I find myself wondering what you're doing here, but more importantly, I find myself wondering how stupid you'd have to be to bring *them* here."

I knew she spoke of the Hunters, who tensed beside me as if her words lashed them.

"Hello, Sibyl."

I gazed at the breathtaking woman before me, trying my hardest to ignore the fact that we were seriously outnumbered here. I couldn't place her accent, but power radiated from her in waves. She was clearly the leader—and the oldest vampire I had ever encountered. I had to fight the urge to bow before her. I wasn't sure where the inclination originated, but it was there, and it was nearly impossible to ignore.

Her dark hair hung wildly from her shoulders in uncontrollable tight curls. She shifted. Her eyes were a bright neon violet, and her tanned skin was sun kissed and beautiful. I swallowed hard and glanced to Jasik.

"Don't make me ask again, Sebastian." She had yet to glance up at us.

I watched her carefully. Her violet eyes were tense as she focused on her blade.

"Sibyl, love," Sebastian said.

In a movement too quick for even my heightened eyes, she was beside him, her freshly sharpened blade teasing the vein in his throat. She slashed her arm to the right, and he began to bleed.

Without thinking, I grabbed her arm, twisting it around so her blade slid into her back. I felt her tense as blade met bone. I pushed her away, my foot meeting the back of her knees, and she fell to the ground, tumbling forward. I stepped back and drew my seax from its sheath, the Hunters mimicking my daring move.

Sibyl was before me, sliding her weapon from her back. "I'm impressed. I have yet to meet a newborn with such foolish courage."

I twisted my wrist and sliced my seax forward, but my arm was caught midair. Sebastian twisted it back, sheathing my weapon in the process. I stood shocked, without my weapon in hand.

"Don't be an idiot," he whispered, though I was sure they could hear him anyway. "Look around you. These vampires are trained killers. You have no chance."

I swallowed the knot in my throat and shook off my tense muscles. I met their hard gazes.

"Very good," Sibyl said, still watching me.

I refused to turn my gaze from her. She stepped forward, her challenging stare deepening. My legs quivered, and my pulse quickened. I unsuccessfully fought to control them both.

Don't back down, I told myself. Hold her stare. You're powerful, too. Never forget that.

She chuckled and blinked. "Very, very good. You will make one hell of a fighter, Avah Taylor."

I frowned.

"You didn't think you could come into *my* home, *challenge* me, and maintain anonymity, did you?"

"How do you know who I am?"

"The world will know of you, Avah. You are always welcome here." She turned on her heel and faced Sebastian, who stood unwavering beside me. "Sebastian, do not bring another into my home without consulting me first, do you understand?"

"Yes, Sibyl. My apologies, Milady."

I arched an eyebrow. He was changing tactics.

"We have a problem," he added.

Vaguely, I heard the other Hunters re-sheath their weapons.

"Yes, these pathetic excuses for protectors lost their priestess, and now there's a Rogue army awaiting your arrival." *Tsk! Tsk!* Her lips curled into a smile when she faced me again.

"You read my mind," I said defiantly.

"I did. As did the others." She gestured to the other hybrids in the room. The watched me closely. Aside from their violet eyes, they looked so... normal. Why would I think differently? Sebastian and I were pretty normal, too. "You should really learn to shield your thoughts, Miss Taylor."

Shield my thoughts? I looked up at Sebastian. *We begin training. Tonight.* He nodded once.

"My dear, Sebastian is a fine specimen, but he's no teacher. Join us. I shall train you."

I gawked. "You don't even know me."

"I know more than you realize."

"Of course. You're a seer." I cursed my inexperience.

She nodded.

"Are my friends welcome?" I asked.

"No."

"Then I won't be staying."

"You may leave the way you came," she said simply, turning on her heel.

"They can't go outside. You know this."

Though I couldn't see her face as she retreated from us, I was sure she was smirking.

"Sibyl, please," I begged. The words felt odd on my tongue.

She stopped and faced me again.

"You're quite defiant, aren't you?"

"I am." I spoke honestly. My mother used to tell me I was too strong-willed. I didn't think there was such a thing.

She exhaled quickly. "Because your problem will become an even bigger issue if we let this progress, we will assist you in eliminating this army. But that is all. Understand, Sebastian?"

He nodded.

"Very well. *They* can stay the day, but this evening, we leave."

"That's it? What's the plan? There were hundreds. We can't just go in. They'll be expecting that."

"Quiet your tongue, child."

Her words were direct. Sibyl had this amazing ability to make me feel as though I was an inexperienced witch, being chastised by my mother yet again.

"Leave it be, Avah. Sibyl is an expert warrior. She knows what she's doing," Sebastian said as he turned to face the Hunters. "Stay quiet, leave them be, stay out of the way, and you just might make it to dusk."

I glanced over my shoulder. The other hybrids watched me carefully. Glancing at each other, they laughed, shaking their heads and looking away, as if they had conversations only a reader could understand. For a second time today, I cursed my inexperience. What were they thinking?

"We're seriously outnumbered, Sebastian."

Jeremiah nodded, looking from hybrid to hybrid.

"I meant against the Rogues. I think we're safe here... for now."

Sebastian shook his head. "There are more. They're just not here right now." He eyed me cautiously.

They were up there. In the sunlight. I swallowed. When should I tell them that we could be exposed to sunlight without concern? When was a good time to break depressing news to someone? And how exactly could I explain it and not have it sound like I was rubbing it in their faces?

"You should rest. Avah and I will train," Sebastian said to Jasik.

He glanced at me, and I nodded. I needed time with Sebastian, and I knew they were safe even with Sebastian and I gone.

Jasik exhaled quickly. "Fine, but you need to rest, too." He extended his arm, and I grabbed his hand, giving it a slight, reassuring squeeze.

"She's stronger. She doesn't need what you need. She doesn't need as much rest. She doesn't need as much sustenance. She's self-reliant. Remember that." Sebastian looked down, meeting my eyes. "Don't fall weak to your mind's lies, Avah. The habits instilled after decades of human existence no longer ring true. You're a creature of the *night and day* now."

Jasik arched an eyebrow at Sebastian's words, but I ignored him and nodded, my mouth drying at the thought of the power within me. I had so much potential, and I was annoyed that it was always just out of reach.

"Shall we, sugar lips?" Sebastian gave me his wicked sexy grin and stalked down the tunnel that led to our only escape. Apparently, the lady killer had reared its ugly head again.

"I'll be fine," I said to Jasik, pulling him into a long, hard kiss. Breathlessly, I gazed up at him; his eyes burned in hunger... for me.

"What did he mean by that?"

"Who knows?" I shook my head and winked.

Concern still etched his eyes, but he smiled. There'd come a time I'd need to explain myself, but I didn't think that time would be when there were eavesdropping vampires nearby.

"Stay safe, my love." He planted a kiss on my forehead and

pulled away, retreating to his place beside the Hunters.

Reluctantly, I followed Sebastian to the tunnel, throwing a quick glance over my shoulder at the other hybrids. They watched me with wonder. I was sure it was strange for them to see such affection between a hybrid and a Hunter. After all, Sibyl didn't seem too fond of vampires with only one special power and not all four.

I emerged from the tunnel, and Sebastian was there to greet me. He placed a finger to his lips. He pointed toward the cave's entrance—about fifty or so feet above us. Smiling, he pressed his legs against the ground and sprung up. In a flash, he was through the entrance and out of sight. Biting my lip, I mimicked his actions. I was quickly embracing the sunlight. A feeling of warmth washed over me. I exhaled as I stretched my arms out to my sides. Rolling onto my tip toes, I tilted my head back. If I could, I'd hug the sun.

A small chuckle brought me back to reality. I dropped my arms, placed my feet firmly on the ground, and opened my eyes. I gave Sebastian a stern look.

"You look beautiful, Avah. Content. You weren't meant to spend your life in the shadows."

That familiar feeling of lust bubbled within me, and I pushed it down, tearing my eyes from his gorgeous gaze.

"Let's train. We don't have much time," I said.

"Always business. Never pleasure," he teased.

"Which lesson are we on? Five hundred and forty-seven?" Sebastian wasn't the only one who could tease.

"Lesson number two. Let's get that shield up. Sit."

He dropped to his bottom, crisscrossing his legs. I followed suit.

"Good. I've had my shield up, protecting those tantalizing insides of yours."

I groaned and rolled my eyes, though I was secretly thankful he gave me *some* privacy—especially from Lillie.

"Though, I removed it when we got here. I needed Sibyl to see what you saw. It was the only way she'd agree to assist us and not rip our throats out for arriving without an invitation."

My jaw dropped. That was even an option?

"Yes. It was."

Ugh. "Creepy much? Can you stop answering my thoughts, you perv?"

"Baby cakes, I hate to break it to you, but there is nothing creepy about your thoughts. Thus, there is nothing perv-tastic about me."

"Perv-tastic? Really?" I laughed. "Sometimes, it's like you were born in the 1980s and not the…" I realized I had no idea how old Sebastian was.

He gazed at me, our eyes meeting.

"One day, pet. One day you'll learn all my dirty little secrets." He winked. "But not today."

I shrugged, playing innocent, as if I wasn't intrigued by his past.

"You're tense. You need to loosen. Shake it out," he said. I watched as he moved his torso, stretching the muscles, cracking his neck. His shoulders hinged forward and then back.

Again, I mimicked his motions, not sure what else to do.

"Good. Close your eyes and clear your mind. Really, this is no different than magic. You just need to focus. You already have the tools to excel."

I nodded as I closed my mind. Instinctively, I focused on my breath. Once I was comfortable with the sounds of my body, I moved on to Sebastian's. His heart thudded lightly in his chest; his breath came in short, low bursts. I wondered why he chose to breathe. Surely, he had learned to break that mortal habit...

"Concentrate, Avah."

I groaned. I swallowed and started again. But the thought was still there.

I opened my eyes. "I can't focus on anything but your breath."

"Fine. I'll hold it."

"Just tell me why."

"Why what?"

"As if you don't know."

"Mortals would notice if we were walking around and not breathing. Eventually, you'll learn to maintain the habit without letting it consume you."

"Consume? How so?" Now I was intrigued.

"Like when we entered the cave. The water didn't consume you. Your fear of drowning did. In time, you'll learn to displace that fear."

I nodded, stretching my muscles, cracking joints. I exhaled and closed my eyes, attempting to refocus.

I peeked an eye open, and Sebastian was watching me. "Thank you," I said before closing my eye again.

Finally, I was able to move past Sebastian's breathing and expand my senses to the trees and flatlands surrounding us. It had been too long since I last heard daylight wildlife scurrying through their lives. The sound was precious to the ear. I had thought I'd never walk among them again. The pain of that thought began to slowly subside, and I realized that was how Jasik and the Hunters felt at every moment of every day. It was frightening.

I began to sink further into the abyss, picking up sounds from miles away. Voices were distant, quiet, barely audible.

Very good, Avah.

My eyes shot open at the internal intrusion.

"Did I just—"

Sebastian smiled and nodded. "You read my mind."

"*Yes!*" I shouted before I pounced into his lap, engulfing him in a hug.

He laughed into my ear as he held me tightly.

"In time, you'll learn to control it without such pretenses."

I knew I was only able to tap into the ability because of the situation: it was calm, quiet, and I could focus. I wouldn't have those conditions during battle. But I didn't care. I was thrilled that I tapped into one of my vampire abilities: the ability to read minds.

"Sit back and refocus," he ordered, and I quickly obliged. I felt as though it was my birthday. I just wanted more surprises, more presents.

Giddy, I closed my eyes and attempted to reconnect. I could feel a cheeky grin plastered across my face, and I could only guess that Sebastian's face bore a similar resemblance. As my excitement waned, I was able to hear him again.

This time, I want you to focus on your inner strength. It's very important that you learn to completely control your shield before we enter battle.

I nodded in response.

I focused on the essence burning within me. It shined brightly, an iridescent energy source just begging to be tapped into. It swirled in circles within my torso. It was powerful, formidable, and beautiful. It moved from my core and spread throughout my body, seeping into every crevice of my being.

Touch it, Avah.

How? I thought.

You know how. The answers are within you. I'm simply a guide.

I didn't move, didn't open my eyes. I was terrified I'd lose the connection to my inner self. The thought made me shiver. How could I have not connected by now? How did I not see and feel this power source within me? Focusing on my essence, I lightly probed the goddess within me. She was spectacular, defiant, and in control. She was me—everything I was meant to become.

As the iridescent glow completely filled me, I began pulling it, tugging it outward. In a quick burst, I threw my head back, gritting my teeth, and the shimmery glow within me seeped from my aura. I opened my eyes, staring in awe as it surrounded me completely. I sat within the protective bubble and giggled as Sebastian ran his fingers across the outer edge.

Focusing on him, I slowly enveloped him within my protective circle, and he sat back with a wide grin plastered across his flawless face.

"Bloody hell! Well done, Avah! I didn't even have to show you how to shield another. You're a natural."

I beamed up at him, proud of my accomplishment.

"Now, pull it back within you."

I closed my eyes, concentrating on my shield. Slowly, in my mind, it retreated back. It pushed against my physical form. I opened my eyes, bringing my arms before me. I watched my shield withdraw toward me, and it glowed against my aura, which burned a bright yellow. The two twirled together, becoming one, until they no longer glowed. Though I couldn't see them any longer, I knew they were there. I could feel them as they burned against my skin in a protective shield of armor.

I looked up to Sebastian and smiled.

"I can't read your thoughts," he said.

I said nothing. Instead, I imagined my invisible shield surrounding my mind. I lowered it briefly, thinking Sebastian's name, before raising it again.

He gasped, his hand reaching for my chin, raising my gaze to his.

"You are magnificent," he said softly.

I bit my lip. I found it nearly impossible to control the screaming girl within me.

"I'd say you've just about got control of your shield. Congratulations, Avah. That's quite an accomplishment."

I pulled him into a hug and whispered in his ear. "Thank you, Sebastian. This is the first time I've felt... strong, safe."

I quickly pushed him away, baffled by my confession. I stared at my hands as I considered my admission. I felt safe with Jasik and, surprisingly, with the other Hunters. But not like this. This was different. Finally, I felt safe in my own skin. I had been terrified for so long. I feared what I was, what I could do. Now, I knew I could control the power within me. I just needed more practice.

I looked at Sebastian. "What's next?"

"Well," he said, running a hand through his long, sandy-brown hair, "your healing ability occurs naturally; you've now got your shield down. Looks like we need to work on your reader and seer skills, yes?"

"I think I've got reading down. I just need practice. What about seeing? That could be extremely helpful," I said.

He nodded, his hand reaching his jaw as he rubbed his fingertips against the stubble there, as if deep in thought.

"I know I won't be an advanced seer or reader, but can you at least show me how to tap into it?"

"Yes. You'll need to learn eventually, anyway."

"Okay. So what do I do?"

"Honestly, much of the same. It's all about focusing, connecting with the power within you. I know you want me to hand you a list of steps and say that following them will lead to success, but that's not how it works, Avah. The answers you seek will be found within you, within that power source. Your being already knows how to do these things. Your mind just needs to learn them now. Unfortunately, *you* control your mind and what it does and how it thinks. We have to break a lifetime of mortal habits."

"Seems mortality really does screw people over." I chuckled.

"Well, more or less, plum cakes." He winked.

"Let's connect again," I said, eager to see how much I could learn in one afternoon.

※

Sebastian and I crept back into the underground cave, where the vampires slept. As I entered, sets of violet eyes opened, watching me cautiously. I ignored them, refusing to let them ruin my good mood. Sebastian and I trained for hours. I still hadn't gotten complete control of my abilities, but I had seen three future events, read Sebastian's ridiculously dirty mind more times than I wanted to, and maintained control over my shield. I wasn't as powerful as Sebastian, but I was getting there.

I sank beside Jasik, resting my head against his chest, and raised my shield. It encompassed each of us: the Hunters and Sebastian. If I was going to sleep beside an army of blood-thirsty hybrids, I needed to know they couldn't attack us when we least expected a fight.

I closed my eyes, silently praying my shield would remain intact even while I wasn't focusing on it. Images of my early visions with Sebastian flashed before my eyes: death, decay, witches, vampires... I swallowed down the knot in my throat.

Something was coming for us, and it was nearly ready to attack.

EIGHT

His fingers lightly caressed my brow bone, and a small smile formed on my lips. I kept my eyes closed and leaned against his frame. I inhaled deeply, refusing to open my eyes.

"Avah," he whispered as he placed a kiss where his finger had just lingered. "We must awaken, my love." He kissed me again, and I groaned against him.

"It's too early."

His body tensed, and my eyes opened. I looked up to meet his gaze, but his eyes were focused on something behind me.

I turned and faced Sibyl, her eyes glowing wickedly as she grinned down at me. She stood only a few feet from us. I pushed myself off the ground and slowly stood, still meeting her gaze.

What was happening? As my hand grasped the handle of my sheathed blade, her smile grew wider.

"You are something special, Avah," she said, turning on her heel and stalking toward the group of hybrids behind her. Their number had tripled overnight. I silently thanked Sebastian for leading us here—even if I didn't feel completely safe around them. Sibyl wanted something from me, and as long as her shield was securing her thoughts I'd never—

My shield! I looked around. I almost hadn't seen its iridescent shimmer. I smiled, dragging my teeth against my bottom lip as I turned to face the Hunters.

"It stayed up," I said breathlessly. I looked at Sebastian, who had his arms crossed over his chest. His eager smile matched mine. "I didn't have to keep focusing."

"I knew you could do it. You just needed to trust your inner strength," Sebastian said.

I pulled Jasik to me and into a hard kiss.

Lillie groaned beside us, but I ignored her. No one would rain on today's parade.

I jumped into Jasik's arms, my legs wrapping around his waist and nuzzled into the crevice of his neck. I glanced up. Malik smiled softly at me—a rarity for him. I returned the gesture and leapt out of Jasik's arms.

"We have a lot of work to do," I said.

I silently called my shield back, shivering in its wake as it reentered me.

"What's on today's agenda?" Jeremiah asked. His gray eyes were glowing, but soft circles were cast beneath them. Had he kept waking to ensure my shield hadn't faltered? It fell to Jeremiah to maintain a shield around us while we slept. I felt a ping of guilt rise within me. I should have woken him, told him about my shield. We all desperately needed a good night's sleep, and while we had gotten one, Jeremiah didn't.

"There's a coven in northern Washington, just along the Canadian border. We'll find sanctuary there," Jasik said.

"Northern Washington? We're going to backtrack?" Lillie asked.

"We know she was near us in Shasta and that she was somewhere cold. We have friends in Canada and Alaska. We can scout the area. Maybe we'll find something."

"Shouldn't we look into Montana first?" I asked. "We're already here."

"There are no Rogue vampires in Montana," Sibyl interjected.

I faced her. "How can you be sure?"

"Because I own this land."

I knew she didn't mean literally, but there was seriousness to her tone. I was sure she knew every time a vampire stepped foot on Montana soil.

"Maybe Sebastian and I can do another locater spell together," I said, turning back toward the Hunters.

Sebastian nodded, though his eyes were lost in thought. "That could work. We've already made a connection with the initial spell."

"Exactly. Do these friends of yours have supplies? We may need to try the spell more than once."

"Yes, they should be just as stocked as we were," Malik cut in. His tone betrayed an eagerness I had never heard before. He seemed… excited.

"Good. What about them?" I whispered the question, as if that would stop nearby hybrids from hearing me.

"What about us?" Sibyl said. I rolled my eyes and turned back toward her and the hybrids.

"Well, we're seeking refuge among beings you don't take too kindly to. I'm thinking that'll be an issue." My tone came out more harshly than I intended.

"We'll find our own safety nearby."

I nodded. "Good idea."

"I'll stay with them," Sebastian offered, giving me a knowing glance. I nodded and smiled, though I feared for his safety. That realization hit me hard. I wasn't sure when I stopped fearing Sebastian and started caring for him, but it had happened, and I couldn't deny it.

I didn't want the protection of yet another coven to fall into our hands. We were too preoccupied with finding our own high priestess.

No one spoke as we stalked through the woods. The Hunters, Sebastian, and I led the way, while the hybrid army followed in our wake. My skin was crawling, and I kept looking over my shoulder to ensure they were still there. I wasn't sure what I feared more: finding them gone or finding them too close for comfort.

"Relax, Avah," Sebastian whispered. I was sure my antsy behavior was rubbing off on him. "They're not going to hurt you. You're one of us."

"It's not me I'm worried about," I replied, meeting Malik's eyes. He shrugged off my concern and returned to small talk with Jasik.

"Stop!" Sibyl yelled, and instinctively, I froze. The authoritative force in her tone was hard to deny. It took several seconds for me to realize she didn't control me, that I didn't answer to her. I spun around.

"What is it—" Before I could finish, something slammed into

me. I flew backward, crashing into a tree, crumbling to the ground.

"No one move!" Sibyl ordered.

I looked up and stared into the red irises of a Rogue, our noses touching. His hand grasped my hair, yanking my head back. I cried out.

"Hair pulling? Really? Way to take the bitch move," I spat. I yanked the dagger from my hip and dug it into his neck.

He growled in response, as if I'd only just inconvenienced him, and I brought the heel of my palm up in a quick jab. The Rogue faltered, and I escaped his grasp. Before I could land another hit, he was tossed backward, as if he weighed nothing. I grasped Jasik's hand as he lifted me from my crouched position, keeping my eyes on the Rogue, who scrambled to his feet.

"Do not engage," Sibyl ordered, and I glanced at her. I knew she was ordering her hybrid army, not me, and it irked me. How was I supposed to trust her, to work with her?

"Seriously? Thanks for the help."

"If you can't handle one measly Rogue, then you will be of no use to us, anyway."

"Screw you," I spat as I pushed past Jasik.

She smiled in response.

"If you think I can't handle one Rogue," I returned my gaze to my attacker, "especially one who was stupid enough to attack alone against dozens, then you have seriously underestimated me." And I liked it. She knew what I could do in terms of abilities, but she didn't know my inner drive or my years of pre-vampire training. My inner strength had gotten me through tougher jams this.

"Show us, then." She either couldn't or didn't want to hide the amusement in her voice. Whatever her motive, I was frustrated beyond belief.

"You don't have anything to prove," Jasik said, reassuring me. He tried to grab my hand, but I pulled from his grasp. I knew it pained him, but I couldn't handle his ego right now. I had my own to keep in check. And it was quickly escaping me.

I ran toward the Rogue, my feet slapping the cold, frozen ground in frustrated rage, and I couldn't help but notice his lack of care at being completely surrounded. One against fifty wasn't great odds. He brushed off any concern and focused solely on me— almost as if I were his true target all along. I stopped dead in my tracks, skidding to a stop just an arm's reach away from the enemy.

"What are you doing? Attack!" Sebastian yelled, his voice squeaking.

"You're here for me, aren't you?" I asked.

Ignoring my query, he sparred with me. Questions swarmed through my mind; I couldn't kill him... yet. I spun around, his fingertips brushing against my bare skin as he attempted to grab me. He mimicked my twirl, facing me once again.

"Why?" I asked. "Why me?"

He dove forward. This time, he grabbed onto my arm as I attempted to bypass his attack. His nails dug into my skin, drawing blood. I ground my teeth before landing a mean right hook across his jaw. His head flung backward on contact, and he released my trapped appendage. I heard the faint sound of the bones in his neck cracking back into place.

"You're surrounded by hybrids, but you don't want them— you don't even care. Tell me why!" I yelled. My arm tingled, my body's healing abilities nearly overwhelming my senses. The Rogue stood, brushing off his clothes in a sad attempt to dismiss my feeble attacks.

"You're smarter than you look. She didn't think you'd figure it out."

"Do you really think it takes more than half a brain to know something was up?" I asked, folding my arms across my chest. I was offended that *she* thought so little of me.

"Are we really going to talk this out?" Sebastian asked, his jaw nearly scraping against the floor.

"As far as Rogue attacks go, this has been pretty easy. Have you ever thought that *she*," I gave sarcastic air quotes to emphasize my point, "wanted you gone? If not, then *she* doesn't know me very well. I think I can handle one Rogue." I desperately needed to know who *she* was, but I couldn't grovel. He'd never give me the information I needed if I did, and at this point, I wasn't too sure I'd ever get the information I needed by simply beating it out of him. Rogues were ruthless. He'd hold out until death—I was sure of it.

A wicked grin branded his face. "Who said I was alone?"

Bile worked its way into my mouth, but I pushed the sickening feeling down. Twigs snapped in the distance, and I knew they were upon us. I spun around in time to see them emerge from the trees. My eyes darted to each as the Hunters and hybrids tensed, bracing themselves for the attack. Sibyl's standing order to leave us be must've been relinquished, because she dashed forward, shoving her hand into a Rogue's chest and ripping out his heart before moving to the next. I couldn't be sure how many surrounded us. Twenty? Thirty? We were cornered and without time to discuss logistics.

Stupidly, I had turned my back on the Rogue I had been fighting, and I only remembered his presence when he dug his fangs into my neck. I screamed as he drained me in long, hard slurps. The pain riveted through my body, leaving an earth-shattering revulsion in my gut.

"Avah!" Jasik called as my knees collapsed.

The Rogue wrapped an arm around me, pressing my body against his. "You're gorgeous, y'know? Maybe I'll keep you for myself," he said between swallows.

The thought was enough to push down the pain and take control of the situation. I put on my game face, slammed the back of my skull into his nose, and quickly turned in his arms until I faced him. Blood gushed from his face as I ran my fingers through his hair. He gasped at the small show of affection, and inside, I smiled. *Amateur.* I gripped the ragged strands, yanking his head back, and dug my fangs into his neck, recharging.

He tasted bitter but powerful. Before he had the chance to resume control, I twisted my arms until his head snapped, and he fell limp. Copying Sibyl's tactic, I slammed my fist against his chest and dug. I crashed past his rib cage, the small bones in my hand shattering upon impact. I sucked in a sharp breath as the pain coursed through me. Almost as quickly as they broke, my bones began to heal—just in time for me to find the soft tissue of his heart. I ripped it out and tossed the flesh to the ground. I faced my attackers, but found none. In a matter of mere minutes, the Hunters and hybrids had killed them all. For a brief moment, I was elated. Perhaps we really did have a chance to save Amicia.

"Nice tactic, though arousal has never been an option for me on the battlefield," Sibyl said.

I shrugged in a sad attempt to hide my embarrassment. "Felt like a good plan at the time. Plus, it worked." I couldn't bear to look at Jasik.

"Death by boner. I like it, A." Jeremiah laughed and gave me a playful slug.

I rolled my eyes but couldn't stop the smile from forming.

I wiped my bloody hand on nearby grass as hybrids effortlessly tossed bodies into a pile. With the snap of her fingertips, Sibyl set them on fire. I let my eyes linger as I wondered if I'd ever have her strength, her confidence, her control. She fought with ease, each move elegantly executed. Watching her attack was no different than watching a ballet dancer perform. She was graceful, nimble, formidable. I promised myself I'd train until I matched her strength.

"So someone's after Avah again?" Lillie asked.

I shrugged. "I'm not worried about it. They don't seem to be too smart." I played it cool, even though I felt like screaming. Was there ever going to be a time I wasn't some pretty prize?

"Or maybe they just didn't expect us," Sibyl countered.

I knew she was right. The hybrid species kept to their secluded lifestyle so much so that Jasik, at nearly seven hundred years old, had only heard stories about another vampire species. He hadn't seen a hybrid in the flesh until I turned.

"Whatever it is, I'm not worried about it. If they're coming, they're coming. Me stressing isn't going to change that. I'd rather focus on Amicia."

I cringed as I recounted the faceless victims sprawled at my feet. I didn't believe in coincidences. Something was coming for me, and I knew *she,* whoever *she* was, had to be tied to it.

CHAPTER
NINE

The mansion looked eerily familiar. Its uncanny decor and location mirrored Amicia's manor perfectly—even the house's layout was identical. I raised a questioning eyebrow when I caught Jasik staring.

"We have good relations with the vampires of this house. When it was time to move and build, we collaborated." He shrugged, as if that was normal behavior.

"Isn't that kinda weird?" I asked.

"No," he said matter-of-factly.

"My guess is our bedrooms aren't the same," I said with a wink.

He smiled his award-winning grin, and my heart skipped a beat. I bit my lower lip, enjoying Jasik's relaxed side. Too often, I didn't see his playful nature. I hoped that would change once

Amicia was brought home.

"We'll be staying in the guest quarters. You and I will share a room." He licked his lips, his cool blue eyes darkening.

I sucked in a sharp breath. "I love your dirty mind." I stood on my tiptoes, and he brought his mouth down, his lips teasingly grazing mine.

"Jasik, I'm so happy you've made it."

Groaning at our lack of physical contact, I stepped back and watched the speaker take each step down the stairs toward us. She moved with finesse, her long, red locks twisted in curls that hung across her chest. Her baby blue eyes watched me carefully as she took Jasik's hands in hers and placed a kiss on either cheek. She did the same to Malik, Lillie, and Jeremiah. When she reached me, I wasn't sure how to react—so I did nothing. She smiled and offered her hand.

"Katalina Devereux, this house's high priestess. I've been dying to meet you, Miss Taylor, but Amicia likes to keep her vampires to herself." Her smile seemed sincere, so I took her hand in a firm grasp.

"Oh, umm… sorry?" I released her hand, feeling inadequate and uncomfortable under her stare.

She laughed, showcasing perfect teeth. In fact, everything about her screamed model. When she spoke, heads turned. She was tall; to meet her gaze, I had to actually look up, and at five foot seven, I wasn't exactly short. Her six foot frame was thin and lanky, but her elegance screamed power. I was sure she was old—probably not as old as Amicia, but old nonetheless.

"No need to apologize. Amicia and I are good friends. She knows she couldn't keep you from me forever."

"Of course not, Miss Devereux. I'm sure we would have met eventually."

"Please, call me Kat. Everyone does." And with that, she spun on her heel, facing Jasik. "You know where your rooms are, and you're welcome to feed when you're ready."

"Thank you, Milady. We will be staying but a day. We sincerely hope to not be a hindrance."

"Oh, stop." She waved her hand dismissively. "You're always welcome. You know that."

Her eyes flickered back to Malik, and I saw the briefest flash of desire cross his eyes. I was stunned into speechlessness. Malik and Kat? His earlier excitement to visit this specific coven was beginning to make sense...

"It's been too long, Milady," Malik said as he grabbed her hand and brought it to his lips. She quivered—yes, *quivered*—as he placed the lightest of kisses against her skin. "You're as radiant as ever."

Blushing, she withdrew her hand. "You're too kind, Malik."

I nudged Jasik, no one but him noticing. Everyone else was likely too busy drooling over the obvious attraction between Malik and Kat. Or maybe that was just me, because Jasik frowned at me and shook his head.

"I'll leave you to settle, then," Kat said as she stepped toward the foyer's staircase. "If you need anything…" she called over her shoulder before disappearing into what I assumed to be her office. I wasn't an idiot. There was a lingering invitation in her final words. I glanced at Malik, noticing his bright eyes. Yep, he caught it, too.

"Well, it looks like Jasik won't be the only one getting laid tonight," Jeremiah said. "Let's hope I can jump on this bandwagon!"

I barked out a hard laugh, though everyone else scowled. I faced him and shrugged. "I thought it was funny," I mumbled.

Jeremiah winked at me.

"Where are her Hunters?" I asked, looking around. A few vampires lingered, but I hadn't seen a single Hunter.

"Patrolling, I'm sure. A high priestess is missing, visitors have arrived, and an army of hybrids slumbers in the woods. They're likely on edge."

I nodded. It was too easy to forget the shit storm we'd gotten ourselves into. "I'm eager to meet them."

"They're eager to meet you, too."

I rolled my eyes. "*Everyone* seems eager to meet me. It's getting old."

Jasik smiled and grabbed my hand, giving it a reassuring squeeze. "You're different, Avah. Special. Don't forget that. You mean something important—a blending of the species. An alternative to war."

I had never thought about my transition as an alternative to the war, but he was right. There were options. We just had to get other vampires and witches to see it.

"Come. Let's get you clean," Jasik said, pulling me toward the stairs.

"Excuse me? Is that your nice, British way of telling me I stink?"

"No, that's my nice, British way of telling you that I plan to devour every inch of you as soon as we get into our room."

I gasped, but not because of his words. It was the hunger, the love, in his eyes that left me speechless once again.

⌒⌒⌒

The first time Jasik and I were intimate, we were in the shower in my private bathroom. As I stepped into a shower once again, I licked my lips. Water cascaded down his muscled torso, and he playfully shook his head, sending droplets flying. I laughed and reached for him, my hands tracing the rigid curves of his stomach. My eyes danced across his nude body; he was a delicious sight to see: toned, tanned, and tantalizing. My mouth watered as I took him in.

"See something you like, love?" he asked with a wicked grin.

I bit my lip and nodded. "Always."

He grabbed my hand that playfully rubbed his body and brought it to rest against his neck. My other arm followed suit, and I pulled him down. His lips met mine in a passionate embrace. His tongue brushed against my lips, and I opened for him. Deepening the kiss, he devoured my mouth with precision strokes of his tongue. Jasik was a fantastic lover. His mouth, his hands, could do things with just the lightest caress. I'd never experienced anything as passionate or as real before. He groaned as he pulled away. I unsuccessfully attempted to protest by pulling him back to me. He was hard against my stomach, so I reached down to grasp his appendage, caressing his length.

He closed his eyes and braced himself by placing one hand against the tiled wall and the other against the glass door. "Avah," he moaned.

Knowing he was at a disadvantage, I dropped to my knees and took him fully in my mouth. My tongue danced across the tight, veined skin. I opened my mouth wider and swallowed, opening my jaw completely, taking him until he rubbed against the back of my throat.

He inhaled sharply. "Avah…"

His hands were at my hair, rubbing, pulling, guiding me to a speed that made him shiver. With one hand at the base of him, the other rested against his stomach, in time with his rapid breathing, I took him long, hard, and quick. Gazing up at him, my eyes met his; their neon glow burned brightly back at me. He licked his lips, his fangs lengthening as he moaned my name. The thought that I was able to bring down such a god—both in bed and on the battlefield—was exhilarating. He came in long, thick spurts, and I greedily swallowed it down, relishing the thought of being with him like no one else could.

I stood, licking my lips dramatically and moaning, my teeth dragging against the skin of my lower lip.

"You're quite the tease," he said, pulling me into another kiss.

I tasted him again, the act intimate, erotic. I moaned, pulling him closer, the short distance between us too much to bear. I ached to be near him, to feel the rough edges of his body brush against the soft curves of mine. He pulled away, ignoring my groans.

"I admire your enthusiasm, my love, but we have all night. And tonight is yours…"

I dragged my nails against the skin on his back as my core

clenched at his promise—and threat.

"But first, turn. Close your eyes."

I obliged, and the heavenly scent of vanilla filled the air. Slowly, Jasik rubbed his palms against my head, swirling his fingertips in perfect spots. I moaned, leaning against him, allowing him to be my embrace.

"Feel good, love?"

I nodded, and he threaded his fingers through the length of my hair. Lowering his arms, he spread the bubbles against my back, soothing knots I didn't realize had settled there. My breathing slowed as I fell into an abyss of pleasure and relaxation.

"This is almost better than having you in bed," I said.

He released a loud laugh.

"I said *almost*."

"Thank the goddess," he replied as he sank his fangs into my neck.

I gasped, my legs buckling. He wrapped an arm around me, supporting my body when my legs had failed me. I reached back, eyes lidded heavily, and ran my hand through his short hair. I pulled him closer to me, but he backed away.

"I just needed a taste," he whispered against my neck. His tongue ran the length of my wound before it healed.

I groaned. "Not fair."

"And what you did was?" He gave me a mischievous grin.

"Fair to whom?" I smiled.

"Precisely."

"Well," I said as I turned around, "two can play at this game, Jasik." I grinned wickedly, grabbed the bottle of shampoo, and squirted a large pile onto my palm. I rubbed my hands together as tantalizingly as possible, swaying my hips, biting my lip, and moaning his name. Before he could pull away, I brushed my fingers through his hair, lowering to wash his torso. I rubbed along the curves of his arms. He turned, and I washed his back, guiding my hands down the length until I grasped his firm buttock. He gasped as I struck his skin with my hand. I giggled as he turned around and grabbed me by the hips. Instinctively, I wrapped my legs around his waist.

"You don't play fair," he said.

"I know," I admitted.

He stepped back, letting the water run down our curves until we were clean.

Stepping out of the shower, we bypassed the towel rack; wet footprints followed in his wake as he took me to the bedroom and gently laid me down. I shimmied to the head of the bed and rested against the plush pillows. Jasik stood at the foot of the bed and then slowly climbed, on his hands and knees, toward me. The dark, thrilling gaze he gave me almost skyrocketed me into an orgasm. I was breathless, my chest heaving shamelessly as I practically panted over him. He was a beautiful sight to see *with* clothes on. Without them, he was a prime specimen of a man. Chiseled, flawless, strong, he was everything women swooned over. And I was lucky enough to call him *mine.*

"Tonight is all about you, Avah," he crooned. "Your body, your pleasure, your needs…" His British accent was thick as he spoke to me in an irresistibly dirty tone.

He placed delicate kisses along the arch of my foot before softly biting the pad of my toe. I gasped, feeling the action deep in my core. It tingled, and I fought back a moan.

His tongue traced its way along my calf and up to my inner thighs, which brazenly fell open for him. He kissed me softly, sweetly, his tongue stroking delicious circles on my skin. My fangs lowered instinctively, and I moaned his name, arching my back. I pressed the heel of my foot against his bottom, inviting him closer. He obliged.

His tongue found the sensitive nub of my core, and I shook involuntarily as he worked me into an ecstatic void. I cried out as I orgasmed, his name on my lips. He blew teasingly onto the throbbing bundle of nerves, and I shuddered, the promise of another orgasm dangerously close.

"I want you," I whispered, my eyes opening to meet his.

He kissed his way toward my torso, his tongue ringing my navel before sliding against the curves of my stomach muscles. A tremor shook through me as he positioned the thick head of himself at my core. Ever so slowly, he inched himself inside me. When he could go no farther, he grasped my hips, arching my back. Carefully, he pushed again until he was rooted fully within me. I dug my fingers into the bed, scrunching the bedsheets in my fisted hands. Leisurely, he pushed in and out, allowing my body to acclimate to the long, thick intruder. My desire coated him as he slipped in and out, still at an excruciatingly slow pace.

"More," I whispered.

"More?" he asked.

"I need more."

He adjusted his stance, leaving one hand to rest by my head, supporting his weight, while the other kept my back arched. I hiked my hips up as high as I could and wrapped my legs around him, my ankles crossing at his bottom.

"Open your eyes, Avah," he said, and I did. "You're so beautiful."

"I love you," I said. I released the sheets and ran my hands up his arms until they settled at his neck and in his hair.

As he thrust punishingly hard and fast into me, he brought his mouth to mine, muffling my cries. I dug my fingers into his hair, pulling on the roots, and squeezed my legs around him, begging him to inch closer until I wasn't sure where I ended and he began. And he did. He always gave me exactly what I needed. When he sank his fangs into my neck, I orgasmed again, moaning, dragging my fingernails against his back. Unable to control my hunger any longer, I bit him. My throbbing core, his deliciously smooth strokes, and the overwhelmingly sweet taste of his blood on my tongue was too much to bear. My orgasm rippled into another and another, until I could no longer keep track. He released my neck. With closed eyes and my name on his lips, he came long and hard. Our bodies, coated in a fine mist, rested against each other as we regained our strength and allowed our sputtering hearts to calm. His forehead rubbed against mine, and I kissed him feverishly.

"I love you, Avah," he said as he lay beside me. I turned toward him, draping my leg over his. "I love you so much it hurts. It terrifies me."

"It's terrifying?" I asked, unable to hide how much the word hurt me.

His head rolled against the pillow, and he was looking into my eyes. "What I wouldn't do for you, for us... it's terrifying. I've—I've never felt this way before. Not with exes, not with family, not for Amicia. I can't explain it. Every day, I love you more." He turned back, his gaze lingering on the fan blades above us. "I didn't think it was possible to love you more."

I propped myself up on my elbow and traced my fingertips along the curve of his defined jawline.

"I loved you the moment I saw you, you know. That's why I wouldn't—*couldn't*—fight back. You looked at me, and I knew I had to have you. I knew you were meant to be mine."

I fought back the tears that threatened to spill.

"You were so perfect, so brave. You were outnumbered, out-strengthed. You fought with grace, with poise." He closed his eyes, as if he were replaying our first encounter behind closed lids. "You were deliberate in your actions and your duties to your coven. You risked your life to save your cousins. I knew you needed their help, but you didn't risk it. Instead, you risked yourself."

"Jasik…" I whispered. No one had ever spoken of me so fondly. The love and admiration seeping from his mouth were a blessing to my ears.

"And I thought, even if it kills me, I'll protect this girl. I'll save her from this world of darkness—a world you didn't belong in. Your light was so bright. The last time I'd seen something so blinding, I was staring at the sun. I knew no one would understand. Even I didn't understand. But you with your katana, your ruthless attacks, and your witchcraft, you put me under your spell the moment I laid my eyes on you."

I swallowed the lump in my throat. How could I explain what he meant to me? How could I explain that he was just as valuable, that I loved him just as much?

"And now I have you, and all I can think about are all the things in this world that are going to try to take you from me. And…" He shook his head, a hand aimlessly running through his tussled hair. "Nothing's ever brought me to my knees, Avah. Not until you."

He looked at me as a tear slid down the curve of my cheek. He leaned forward and kissed it away.

"I'm yours. Forever," he whispered. He didn't wait for me to reply. Instead, he took my mouth with his and made love to me until the sun set.

∽

"Tired?" Jeremiah asked as I sat down at the table for breakfast. I looked up in time to see him wiggle his eyebrows.

"Surprisingly, no," I replied, ignoring his sexual innuendo.

"Yeah, that's that vampire strength. We really don't *have* to sleep daily. We just do. Habit, I guess. Like breathing."

I nodded as I gulped down the mug of blood set before me.

"So, what's the plan?" Lillie asked, looking from the other Hunters to me.

"I actually have an idea…" I said.

Jasik met my gaze and raised an eyebrow.

"Sebastian and I are going to try another locater spell."

"We already did that. We didn't get anywhere," Lillie stated.

"True, but this time, we have a greater power source," I said with a grin.

"Do you think they'll help?" Malik asked.

I glanced at him, noticing his disheveled appearance. I guessed I really wasn't the only one who got lucky last night. I smiled a cheeky grin at him.

"What?" he asked, as if he didn't know that I *knew*.

I shook my head. "Nothing. Lookin' good." I winked, and he *blushed*. I didn't think Malik was capable of expressing such an emotion—or, really, *any* emotion. He'd always been stiff and straight-forward around me. I was happy someone existed who could make him feel deeper emotions than fight or flight.

He cleared his throat. "I don't know what you're talking about." Sure you don't.

I laughed. "Smooth! But yes, I think they will. Honestly, it's *this,* or we run from place to place and hope to get lucky. My guess is they want to get home as much as we do. And I think they're just as uncomfortable around us as we are around them."

"This is a good plan," Jasik said, rubbing my leg with his hand. Shocks electrified my system at his touch, and I bit my lip. His eyes darkened as they watched me closely. I shook my head in an attempt to clear my thoughts. I had to stay focused on the task at hand.

I knew this plan would work, but I also had ulterior motives. While learning to control my abilities with Sebastian, I was able to see my future—a war that led to our demise. With fifty hybrids lending me their power, I had to have enough strength to see more, to see *who* was coming for us... before it was too late.

CHAPTER
TEN

I stepped outside, embracing the darkness. I inhaled deeply. Kat's coven resided deep within the North Cascades National Park in rural northern Washington State. Though our coven was graced with the Pacific Ocean's salty air, the surrounding woods here reminded me of home. I missed the manor, the vampires. I kicked at the packed snow that crunched beneath my feet as I left the safety of the coven in search of the hybrid army. I knew they were close. I could *feel* them. When they were near, my skin tingled. It was as if everything within me unconsciously reached out to something familiar—something like me.

I found Sebastian sitting alone, his breath released in lacy puffs of steam. As a vampire, I never felt cold, and I was beginning to forget that January in Northern Washington State had to be freezing. Sebastian's back was to me, but I was sure he knew I was there, lingering, staring. I decided to take a seat beside him. I sank against the crunchy ground. We didn't speak; instead, I dug my hands into the snow, balling it between my fists.

I wasn't sure when it happened, but at some point, I released my hatred for Sebastian, and I began to trust him—like him, even. I knew the others still worried about his intentions, but I was sure he wouldn't intentionally hurt us. He reminded me of Jeremiah at times. Both men hid behind their jokes, their looks, their women, but sometimes, when they thought no one was looking, I'd see it. A flash of longing, of loneliness in their eyes. They both wanted so much more than what they had at their disposal.

I tossed the ball of snow in the air, catching it again. Sometimes, it seemed like I could sit in silence forever. The witches made me believe I was born to be some chosen vampire hunter, but in reality, I was born to be a vampire: secluded, alone, in darkness. I found peace there. I dropped the snowball and found Sebastian staring at me intently.

"Hmm?" I asked, suddenly feeling self-conscious under his heavy-lidded gaze.

He shook his head and looked away. I kept staring at him, reflecting on his chiseled looks. He reminded me so much of Jasik. Both had their brooding down, both were incredibly sexy, and both looked at me with an intensity that made my heart flutter.

"When this is over, I want you to stay with us." I spoke barely above a whisper. In fact, I spoke so quietly, I wondered if I had even said it aloud. And then he looked at me.

"Avah—"

"No, don't overthink it."

"I don't belong here. Neither do you…"

I exhaled sharply. "Not this again."

He shook his head but said nothing.

"Sebastian, I care for you. I want you to stay. We can make this work." I grabbed his hand, offering a light, reassuring squeeze. He squeezed me back with a ferocity that made me gasp. His fingers linked with mine.

"This feels right," he said softly.

"I know." I couldn't deny the connection we had. It left me with so many questions I didn't think either of us could answer. Did we feel this way because he saved my life that first night we met? Was it because he was my link to learning more about who I was? Or was it more? What I felt for Jasik was different, stronger, but my feelings for both men were undeniable.

"Please tell me you'll stay," I whispered. Ignoring the sparks that shot through my skin as the pad of his thumb rubbed against my hand.

"Please don't ask me to lie to you, Avah," he said without looking at me.

I swallowed hard. In that moment, I realized just how much Sebastian meant to me. My heart ached at the thought of losing him.

"Will you think about it?" I asked, my voice breaking.

There was a long pause before he said, "Yes."

I smiled and placed a shaky kiss against his cheek. He turned, his nose brushing against mine as I began to pull away. I froze, my eyes lingering on his lips. He was close, so close. His heart beat rapidly in my mind. The loud thumping was numbing. His breathing became heavy as we shared the air between us. He leaned forward, placing his lips against mine, and I didn't pull away. I closed my eyes, allowing myself to indulge in his soft lips. Dropping my hand, he placed his fingers at the base of my spine, and I brought mine to run through his hair. Our kiss deepened, and my heart fluttered.

I fell into a darkness, a void of longing. I missed him. I missed him so much—even though I'd just had him. He tasted differently, smelled differently, felt differently, but I ignored the concern filling my gut as my tongue brushed against his. My teeth dragged against his lower lip, and he moaned in response. My name was on his lips, and his Australian accent ripped me out of my dream and back to reality.

This wasn't real. He wasn't Jasik. I didn't want Sebastian in that way.

I pulled away, shuffling ungracefully on my feet. I stood on shaky legs, my fingers grazing the skin of my swollen lips. I shook my head, looking down at him as he remained seated.

"I can't... I can't be with you like this, Sebastian."

He groaned and stood. "Why? You feel something for me. I know you do. Just admit it!" His eyes glowed brightly—from anger or arousal, I wasn't sure.

"I do. I..." I looked at the ground, as if the words I needed to find were sprawled at my feet. "I—I think I'm starting to love you..."

He gasped and took a step forward, closing the distance between us.

"No!" I said, placing my palms against the tight muscles of his chest.

"Avah, I feel the same way. Stop fighting this. Stop fighting *us*."

"You didn't let me finish," I said as I stepped backward. I kept my arms outstretched, a silent reminder to stay back.

"I do love you. At least, I think I do. But I don't love you the way I love *him*."

"How do you know it's not just some sick sire bond with him?" he spat.

I cringed. "It isn't. I just know it. I can *feel* it."

He shook his head, running a hand through his hair.

"I love you like family, Sebastian. You're like... I don't know. The brother I never had." The thought made me squirm. I rubbed at my lips. I could still taste him; my lips were still moist.

Pain flashed before his eyes as he registered that he and I were *never* going to happen the way he wanted us to.

"But I still need you in my life, and I know you need me in yours. Think about it, Sebastian. Think about how you really feel about me. Sure, there's a physical attraction, but there's *more*. I know you feel that, too."

His arms fell to his sides. "We should probably talk about the plan for today."

"Sebastian," I said softly, "don't change the subject."

"There's no point in continuing, Avah. There's no us. You've made that clear. So let's just move on."

"Fine. But this discussion isn't over." I gave him my no-nonsense tone and hoped he'd take it seriously.

His eyes met mine, and I swallowed hard. He was hurt, but underneath that, I saw recognition. I knew he just needed time. I still hadn't learned about Sebastian's past, but I was sure it'd been a long time since he'd cared for someone or had someone to care for him. This was new to him. He needed time to understand his feelings.

"Well, I was thinking we could try another locater spell. We're closer now. Not sure if that'll help, but we also have the hybrids. I was thinking we could link, use their power, just enough to make contact. Think they'll go for that?"

"Yes," he said without hesitation.

"You seem sure."

"I am. I spent all night with them. They want this over with just as much as we do. We all want to go home, Avah."

His words stung. "Home," I said. "Where is home?"

He didn't answer. Instead, he turned on his heel and began walking away. "I'll find the others, let them know the plan," he said over his shoulder.

I didn't chase him. I just let him go. He needed time, and I couldn't risk pushing him away. Eventually, he'd see what I saw. He had to.

I turned back toward the manor and froze. Jasik sat on the steps that led to the wraparound porch. He looked... defeated. I knew he'd not only witnessed the encounter, but he was close enough to hear everything, too. My heart sank as I thought about the pain I'd just put him through. I couldn't imagine seeing him with someone else.

"I'm sorry," I said as I took the stairs. I wrapped my arms around my chest, as if they could protect me from whatever would happen next.

"Don't."

"Jasik, please—"

"I said don't." He paused; the seconds passed by excruciatingly slowly as I waited for him to finish. "Don't be sorry. I... understand. He's like you, Avah. He can give you... more."

My words from last night echoed in my mind. I had practically begged him for more.

"I need more of you, not him."

"You don't know that."

"I know he doesn't really love me. At least, not like how you love me."

He swallowed hard, his Adam's apple bobbing in his throat.

"For the past few days, I've felt like... like you're not telling me something. Was this it? Was this what you've been hiding?"

"No! I'm not hiding... this. I wasn't hiding this, because there's nothing going on between Sebastian and me to hide."

He didn't speak. He didn't need to. He knew I was keeping secrets, and while I hated doing that, I wasn't sure now was the time to admit all wrongs. Knowing I could eat real food and go out into sunlight would only back up his claims that he can't give me what I need. I needed him to see that I was happy, that what we had was perfect. I didn't need anything more.

"Jasik… I don't know what to say." Tears burned behind my eyes.

"Avah… I just…" He exhaled sharply, running a hand through his tousled hair. "I don't want to lose you." His voice came in a whisper, so soft I wondered if he hadn't actually said what I begged to hear.

When I didn't say anything, he looked up at me. Pain flared behind his icy blue eyes.

I stepped forward, pushing him back, and straddled his lap. I pulled him close to me, resting my head against the curve of his neck. His pulse was quick, steady. I kissed the throbbing vein, and he gasped as I let my teeth graze the sensitive skin.

"No one can take me from you, Jasik. No one. Not ever. I'm yours… forever." I pulled away to look at him.

His hand ran through the length of my hair as he brushed it from my eyes. I stared into his eyes as I let the tears slowly fall.

"Do you really think I feel any differently about you than you feel about me?" I asked as he brushed away my tears. "I don't want to lose you, either. I can't—I can't imagine a life without you."

He pulled me close, kissing my temple. Our rapid breathing caused our chests to pump in unison. Everything about Jasik was right, perfect. We were made to love each other. The love I felt for Sebastian was different. Familial. The love I felt for Jasik was powerful, effortless, forever.

"That night, we were destined to meet, to be together. I've waited my whole life for you, Jasik."

He chuckled. "I've waited nearly seven hundred years for you."

I smiled and inhaled deeply, enjoying being near Jasik. He smelled of mint, vanilla, and his own unique musk.

"I'm so sorry," I said.

I leaned in and placed a weak kiss on his lips. He pulled me closer, deepening our contact, and I relished in being with him in a way I couldn't bear to lose.

"Fiends!" Jeremiah said as he stepped onto the porch. "Man, what vitamins are you taking? Seriously. All morning *and* all night?"

I barked out a loud laugh and stood on wobbly legs. "You're such a perv, Jeremiah. Y'know that?"

He waggled his eyebrows and winked at me. "The ladies love it."

CHAPTER
ELEVEN

"**A**re you nervous?" Sebastian asked. His cool, confident demeanor showed no signs of our earlier indecency. It was almost as if it had never happened. I could only take that as a good sign. Maybe he was realizing that I meant to him the same thing he meant to me?

"A little," I said as we stalked closer to our goal.

"Don't be. You'll do fine."

"It's the first time since—"

"I know."

"Well, not really the first. There was one other time, and it didn't go so well." I swallowed the knot forming in my throat.

"Relax. You're tense. And put your sunglasses on. We're close now."

I obeyed his command, watching as he removed his sunglasses from his head and put them on.

"Jeez, Avah. You're shaking. Calm down." He wrapped an arm around my shoulder and pulled me close to him. I tensed under his touch, and he dropped his arm back to his side. "Sorry."

I shook my head. "Don't be. I'm just…"

"You're nervous, and rightfully so."

I kicked the gravel and chunks of salt at my feet as the frozen blades of grass turned to pavement. The street was empty, and I found myself offering a silent prayer in thanks. Sebastian had done research while everyone slept. It still baffled me that he had the same idea I had. Somehow, we got on a wavelength that left us finishing each other's thoughts. If I weren't an undead shadow worshipper who enjoyed sipping on blood and intimacy with my almost seven-hundred-year-old boyfriend, I'd find that to be creepy.

There was only one metaphysical shop in town. In order to complete our locater spell successfully, we needed to stock up on some supplies. The vampire coven we were staying with had the same supply room in the basement, but they were running low on too many important ingredients. Today was our only chance to get supplies in order to complete the spell before the sun rose.

"That's it," Sebastian said, pointing to a corner store. It was brick and shared the building with a bookstore and cafe. Across the street was a small Catholic church. I smiled at the thought of a religious institution being so close to a Wicca store.

"What's so funny?" Sebastian asked, giving me a small smile.

"There's a church across the street," I said, tilting my head in a point.

"Ha! Think they ever stop by?" He winked.

"I bet protesting is a regular event." I laughed.

I shook my head, and my heart sank. My smile escaped me, leaving a frown in its wake. They turned the corner and were nearly face to face with us. Only an arm's reach away, they overloaded my senses. I shivered, my fangs lowering at the thought of the blood coursing through their veins. I stopped, watching them closely. There were five. Two men and three women. They laughed, and the girls wobbled in their heels. Inhaling deeply, I closed my eyes. They were drunk. The smell of alcohol made my throat constrict. I fisted my hands at my sides. My nails dug into my palms, drawing blood. I focused on my scent, forcing myself to ignore the human presence. Before I allowed myself to reopen my eyes, I waited until I could no longer hear their drunken chat and clanking feet. A door slammed, muffling their voices, and a car started, speeding away.

I opened my eyes and found Sebastian gazing down at me, a cheeky grin on his face. "I'm proud of you."

"Yeah, thanks for the help." I pretended to be annoyed, but really, I wasn't. I was proud of myself, too. Everything inside me told me to react on my predator instincts. Ignoring them wasn't an easy task.

"You didn't need help, and you need to stop thinking that you do. You're strong enough to handle anything life throws at you. You just need to believe in that, in yourself."

I smiled and brought my palms before me. Having already healed, they bared no marks. "Let's just get this over with."

"Sounds good to me. I'm surprised lover boy didn't insist on coming. Naturally, we'd run into humans," he said.

I glanced up at him, and his face betrayed the pain of acknowledging my relationship with Jasik. "Maybe he trusted you to get me through it," I said in an attempt to smooth things over. I needed Jasik and Sebastian to become friends for the long haul.

Pfft! Sebastian rolled his lips in disbelief.

"Sebastian, he does trust you. If he didn't, you'd never be alone with me. Besides, I think you've proven yourself more times than not since that first night."

In reality, Jasik had told me he had a meeting to attend to, and I didn't ask any questions. I was just happy, after what had happened, he trusted me—and Sebastian—enough to let us go to town alone together.

"Yeah, to you. No one else—"

"Stop. They care, too. Lillie even let you *feed* from her. That's not something taken lightly, as I'm sure you know… unless you're Jeremiah." I was sure blood and sex went hand in hand for him.

"Their opinions don't matter."

My jaw clenched. If we were going to stick together *as friends*, he'd have to stop putting me on this pedestal. I told myself he just needed more time. When this was all said and done, he'd realize he cared about them, they cared about him, and we could all live together… forever.

Sebastian grasped the doorknob to the shop and stepped aside to let me in. Instantly, we were bombarded with the familiar scent of sage. I closed my eyes and inhaled deeply.

"Mmm, now there's a smell I miss," I said with a smile.

"Guess it's not so bad," Sebastian admitted.

"Welcome!" a voice called from the back of the store. "We're only open for another fifteen minutes, but I'm happy to help you find what you're looking for." With each word, the voice grew louder, closer, until the young store clerk stood just before us. She was young, but her power seeped from her pores. When she finally looked at us, her entire body stiffened as she took us in.

She knows, I thought.

I know, Sebastian replied, and I jumped. His voice in my head was still something I'd have to get used to.

"How…" She shook, taking a step backward. "How did you get in here?"

"We won't hurt you. We just need a few supplies. That's it."

She began to convulse; her breathing became erratic. A fine layer of mist coated her paling skin.

"Jeez, you're going to faint. Calm down," Sebastian said. His long strides eliminated the space between them with just a couple steps. He grabbed onto her arms before she could flop to the floor.

She screamed a piercing shriek that made me jump.

"Did you hurt her?" I asked as I ran to her side.

"What? No!" he yelled. "I barely touched her!"

"Shh. It's okay," I said, running a hand across her temple, pushing back the hair that stuck to her skin with sweat.

"I… can't… breathe," she said between hiccuped breaths.

"Look at me. Focus. Breathe with me. Breathe in," I inhaled a long, slow breath, "and breathe out," I said as I released an overly dramatic breath. I repeated the words and process another four times before her pulse finally slowed. "You're okay. What's your name?"

"I—I'm… I'm…"

"I'm Avah, and this is Sebastian, and we are not going to hurt you. I promise." I flashed her an bright smile. "But you don't have to tell us your name. We just need to buy a couple things. Can you tell us where you keep these items?" I handed her a folded piece of paper with scribbled herbs, crystals, and more listed.

She nodded, never letting her gaze leave mine.

"Why…" She shook her head.

"Hmm?"

"Why are you wearing sunglasses? It's night."

Sebastian laughed. "You have the opportunity for a tell-all, and that's your first question? Our designer eye-wear?"

His Australian accent was thick and coated the words in a sexy hug. I arched an eyebrow. *She's, like, seventeen. Stop putting on the moves.*

He gawked at me before his mouth settled in a firm line. *Jealous?*

I rolled my eyes.

"Umm… I just, I don't know," she said as she stood.

She was still shaking, so I took a step back. I gripped Sebastian's arm and yanked him back, too, since he obviously was missing her fairly obvious fear. She glanced at the list and then looked back at us. She did it again and again, reading one item and then making sure we were still far enough way to make her semi-comfortable before moving on to the next.

"If you want, we can wait outside or by the door or something. I trust you'll get all the items, and I have cash. You can keep it all."

Her hands shook as she stared at me without speaking. It seemed like hours were passing as she contemplated my offer.

Finally, she swallowed and said, "Why are you being nice to me?"

I smiled at her. "Because we're nice people."

"You're not *people*. I know what you are."

"Technicality. We *were* nice people, and that demeanor hasn't changed. I told you we don't want to hurt you, and I mean it. We just need those items."

She nodded and looked at the list again. "Why do you need these items?"

"We're doing a locater spell. A friend of ours, she's missing."

"How did you find a witch to help you?" she asked, her eyes wide.

"It's not what you think," I said, imagining her mind was picturing a coven being ambushed and witches being tied up, forced to practice magic for us.

"Okay… Just, wait by the door, and don't move. My element is fire. I will use it."

I nodded and stepped back until I pushed up against the door. I crossed my arms over my chest and stayed still, showing her I would comply. Thankfully, Sebastian did the same, his eyes never leaving her. She busied herself by grabbing ingredients and tossing them in a small bag as she went through each item on the list.

After grabbing an item, she'd look over her shoulder, and I smiled again. After a few times, she returned my motion with a hesitant smile.

"She likes you," Sebastian whispered.

"*You* like her," I said matter-of-factly.

He narrowed his eyes at me. "I told you, I don't—"

"Do witches? Yeah, yeah. Then stop staring."

"You're staring," he countered.

"Not like you." I enjoyed our bickering. It was as if we were already family.

"Here," she said, rolling the top of the paper bag before tossing it to me. Sebastian caught it in mid-air. "Now leave. Please."

"Thank you," I said as I turned on my heel, opened the door, and stepped aside for Sebastian. He had stepped outside and took a few long strides toward home when I realized I didn't pay her. I spun around. "Oh! Wait!" The door shut behind me, entrapping us together.

She had already begun walking away, but I quickly walked toward her, and she turned and flinched like I'd hit her. Her arm lashed out as she yelled a word that was too familiar for comfort. I was engulfed in flames, lit by the spark of her fire magic. I dropped to my knees, screaming as the fire ate at my skin. The pain overtook my senses, my mind. I could think of nothing but the fire burning away my existence.

A wash of water poured over me, and I fell back into Sebastian's arms. He held me gently. My body shivered as it slowly began to heal. I was sticky, wet, and smelled of burnt hair and skin.

"Sebastian," I whispered. I knew he had used his ability to control water to put out the fire—even though that risked exposing our kind to this witch and, in turn, her coven. I raised my hand, pushing his sunglasses from his eyes, and the skin of my arm peeled off, sticking to the floor. I cried out, my arm falling limply back to the ground.

"Shh, don't move. Don't move. You're going to be okay," he said, placing a light kiss against my scalp. He began rocking back and forth, and only then did I realize his eyes were misty. How close had I come?

"So… thirsty," I said. My body felt heavy, weak. My fangs were exposed, and my eyes burned where the plastic of my sunglasses had melted against my skin.

"I know, sugar. But you have to wait. I can't move you yet." His voice was filled with concern.

Rolling my head, I glanced down. I gritted my teeth as I felt the skin on the back of my neck rip off and stick to Sebastian's arm. I gasped at the sight. Where my skin wasn't bubbling, it was just… gone. Instead, I saw the red, swollen flesh that skin was supposed to hide from prying eyes. Most of my flesh had charred, turning black as it cooked in the flames. My clothes were nearly gone. Only a few scraps had covered my body. Chunks of skin and fried hair decorated the store's floor around me. I glanced up; the store clerk witch was gone.

"I just… wanted to pay…" I said breathlessly.

"I know, baby. I know. Don't talk. It takes too much energy. You need to heal, and then we'll feed."

"Can't wait. Need it now." My body was excruciatingly heavy. As a vampire, I felt light, carefree, as if I was always a mortal swimming, but now, I felt like I'd emerged from the water and was no longer weightless. I couldn't bear to hold on; the pain was cutting through to my core. It nestled deeply within me—and stayed there.

He exhaled quickly and said, "Close your mouth. Bite your teeth together. I don't want you to rip your tongue apart."

Unsure, I still obeyed. Quickly, he shifted so his arm was free from my weight. I cried out between clenched teeth, feeling the now familiar sensation of my tissue being ripped from my bones. In a swift motion, Sebastian bit into his wrist and offered it to me. I couldn't move, so he hovered the steady stream over my mouth. He healed, and he repeated the motion. Over and over again, he offered me his life, healing only seconds later and then ripping into his flesh again.

"No more," I said. "You need your strength, too."

"I don't care about me, Avah. You still look—"

"Awful, I know." I closed my eyes.

"Your hair is growing back," he said, and I could hear his smile.

"Thank the goddess for that," I snickered.

"You must be feeling better. Can't say you look much better, though."

"I get it. I look like crap. Stop reminding me." I kept my eyes closed, unwilling to acknowledge this close call with death.

"Bloody hell. What the bugger do you want?" Sebastian growled, and my eyes jerked open in time to see his shield surround us. It was our only defense. Sebastian couldn't move without ripping off more skin, and my strength was dwindling. I couldn't take another hit and survive.

"I'm... I thought she was going to kill me." The store clerk carried spare clothes and a bottle of water. She set them down just outside the shield.

"She was going to pay you!" he yelled.

"I—I'm sorry."

"Yeah, well, now you're not getting paid. And we're still taking the supplies! You burnt the money. That's not our problem."

If I had more strength, I would have laughed at Sebastian's attempt to *best* her in this situation.

"Please, take them. Take these, too. Keep them."

"Thank you," I whispered.

"Yeah, it's the least you could do," Sebastian spat.

"Look, I said I was sorry! Have you forgotten that we're enemies? I didn't have to help you!"

"Stupid, brain-washed child," he said as he shook his head.

My breath caught. "Don't," I said, willing him to not expose the secret that had left me an outcast. This girl didn't have to worry about being chosen. She didn't need to know that her family had been lying to her all her life.

"Relax, baby girl," he said, his features instantly softening when he looked at me. "You need to feed again. Here." I closed my eyes again.

He placed his wrist to my mouth, and my fangs tore through his flesh. He rested against my lips, the pain there now gone, and I took long, greedy swallows. My body began to tingle as its healing magic worked to fix the hot mess I was in. The pain subsided until I couldn't feel it any longer.

I heard Sebastian inhale sharply, and my eyes shot open in time to see him quickly look away. I released his wrist and glanced down. I lay nude in his arms, my skin flawlessly untouched. I felt my cheeks heat as I sat forward. One arm draped over my breasts while the other rested against my upper thighs. Sebastian gripped my arms and moved from underneath me. He lowered his shield just enough to quickly grab the garments she left for me. He set them beside me, his eyes never lingering. He stood again, crossing his arms, and faced the girl. I was sure it was an alpha staring contest, but I didn't care. I dressed quickly in the jeans and t-shirt before resting a hand on Sebastian's back. His tensed muscles relaxed as he turned to face me. I pulled him in a hug, squeezing him against me as I let tears fall.

"That was too close," I said.

"I know. Goddess, do I know."

I pulled away and rested my forehead against his. With my eyes closed, I regained my composure; he wiped away any evidence of a breakdown.

"We need to go, darlin'," he said.

I nodded and leaned against him, still weak. Everything I had went into healing my body. I needed to feed... badly. "I don't think I can go out there and not hurt someone." I swallowed hard.

"Don't worry about that. I won't let you hurt anyone." His thumb traced the curve of my cheek. "I promise."

The witch gasped, but I ignored her.

I nodded. "Can you carry me? I feel—"

"Yes. Come," he said, and I fell against him completely. He grasped an arm under my knees and cradled me against him. My eyelids were heavy, and I knew darkness would soon consume me. I heard the faint crinkling of the paper bag and muffled apologies from the store clerk before the bell on the front door rang. The wind danced across my skin as Sebastian took me home.

"Sebastian," I whispered.

"Yes, I'm here, baby girl. We'll be there soon."

"Don't tell—"

"I won't. I'll leave that to you. I don't need lover boy to hate me even more than he does."

I smiled. "You like him. Admit it."

"Maybe a little."

"I knew it." I smiled, nuzzling closer to his chest.

"He's good for you," he admitted.

"He really is."

"Yeah, well, I figured you won't even remember this tomorrow."

I replayed his words over and over in my mind, willing myself to remember his admission, until there was nothing but silence.

CHAPTER
TWELVE

I grunted as I opened my eyes. My body felt heavy, as if I'd slept for days on end. An arm slid around me, and I glanced down. I was still wearing the jeans and t-shirt. I smiled at the familiar presence of Jasik's muscular arm pulling me closer toward him. Pushing my hair back, he pressed a kiss to the sensitive skin behind my ear.

"Avah, love," he whispered, his breath tickling my skin. My shoulders rolled as I shivered at the sensation. I turned to face him. I'd never get tired of staring into his crystal clear blue eyes. Their usual neon glow was gone; today, they were hauntingly dark.

I pressed a kiss to the peak of his nose and pulled him into a tight hug. He nuzzled into my neck and inhaled deeply.

"Sebastian told you…"

He nodded.

I shook my head. "I wanted to tell you. I told him not to say anything."

He pulled away and frowned. "He didn't have a choice. It was obvious something had happened. You returned in his arms, unable to walk or wake, and your attire was different. We drew our own conclusions and gave him no choice but to explain himself." I knew Jasik referred to both himself and the other Hunters when he said *we*. My heart leapt at the thought of their immediate defense of me. I was used to Jasik's emotional connection, but not the others'.

And then his words hit me. I gasped. "It was... He didn't do this. He *saved* me. I—I would have died." I swallowed, my throat dry.

His jaw clenched. "I know," he whispered. "He told me about the girl, the fire, how close it was." He closed his eyes. "I should have been there..."

"Jasik, no. Don't do this. It's not your fault, either. Two hybrids weren't enough. It was just... a close call. One of many I'll have in the expanse of forever, I'm sure."

He opened his eyes. "Too close."

"I know," I admitted. "But I'm here now, and I'm okay. How long have I been out?"

"Only a day. It's time to wake."

I nodded and released him from my grasp. I stood on weak legs. "I need to feed."

"Again?" he asked, surprised.

"What do you mean?"

"You fed from Sebastian. Twice," he looked down, crossing his arms, unable to meet my gaze.

"Jasik—" I walked toward him, willing him to understand that it wasn't a sexual experience. "It wasn't like us. It was survival. That's all I thought, felt. He didn't feel anything, either."

He nodded his understanding. I was sure jealousy was a new emotion for him. "You also drank bagged blood, and you fed from me all night."

"I did?"

"I'm not surprised that you don't remember. You weren't well. You were in a daze, in and out of consciousness. Whenever you woke, even if for the briefest of moments, I made sure I was there to give you whatever you needed."

"Jasik," I whispered, "that was dangerous. I could've taken too much. You could've—"

"It doesn't matter. If you weren't going to survive, I wasn't, either." His tone betrayed his pain and no-nonsense attitude.

I pressed a kiss to his lips. "Thank you." It was done, in the past. There was no reason to argue now. Besides, I would have done the same had the situation been reversed.

"Have you not yet realized the power you have over me? For you, my love, I'd give my life," he said.

∽

The dining area was eerily quiet as I walked in and took a seat at a table the Hunters and Sebastian occupied.

"How are you feeling?" Malik asked. I was surprised he was the first to speak. I knew he cared for me, but only because I was with his brother. More times than not, he gave me the impression he'd have no care for me if Jasik and I weren't together. Jasik held my hand under the table, his thumb lightly brushing over my skin.

"Better, thanks." I smiled to reassure the group. "And I'm ready to do the locater spell." I looked at Sebastian.

He opened his mouth but snapped it back again. He was going to argue, but my glare spoke volumes.

"We don't have time to mess around. I'll refuel, and then we're starting. Have you spoken with Sibyl?"

He nodded. "They're available if we need them, but she thinks we should try alone first." He shrugged.

"Works for me. I'd like to see if we can reach her alone, anyway." A vampire dropped two full mugs of blood in front of me, and I looked up to thank her.

She placed a comforting hand on my shoulder and said, "I'm glad you're okay, Avah."

"Umm, thanks," I said as she turned to walk away. "Who was that?"

"Girl, everyone knows what happened. Everyone. Pretty sure Kat will be down soon, too. When Sebastian showed up with you lookin' the way you did…" Jeremiah shook his head, his knuckles turning white as he grasped his mug a little too hard. "He's lucky *all* we did was make a scene. *We* take care of our own." He glared at Sebastian, who was completely oblivious to Jeremiah's mood change. I reached across the table, grasping Jeremiah's hand in my own. His eyes met mine, and he gave me a wink. I pulled away, smiling.

When I was still a witch, I had regularly patrolled our property in search of lingering vampires. I usually didn't have any trouble finding them, but one time, I nearly died in the fight. I was alone, stupidly, and it took all of my strength to reach home before succumbing to the blood loss. The vampire had impaled me with my own weapon. When I reached my house, my coven cleaned my wound and performed a healing spell. Afterward, my mother punished me by spelling the house so I couldn't leave for weeks. Her only care was that I was endangering my *chosen* status. She called my behavior reckless, amateur, and unacceptable—even though *she* sent me on hunts and ordered me to slay vampires. Closing my eyes, I could still hear her screams. Not once did she ask if I was okay. Not once did she pull me into a hug and cry. I knew she was playing her role of our coven's high priestess. She couldn't show weakness—not even for her own daughter. It strained our relationship, but it also made me the fighter I was today.

As I glanced around the table, I saw a vast array of emotions on the Hunters' faces. I wasn't used to displays of love or concern. My heart ached at the thought.

"I think everyone's just surprised you survived. Sebastian gave us the gory details thanks to Jasik's persuasion." Lillie glanced at the two vampires before returning her eyes to me. "I'm really happy you're both okay." She smiled. Rarely did I see this side of Lillie. We didn't have the best start, because she had lingering feelings for Jasik that weren't returned. But she was moving on, letting go, and accepting us as a couple. Slowly, she was opening up to me, and I was thrilled. If I was going to live an eternity, I'd need a girlfriend.

"Thank you." I reached out and grabbed her hand, giving it a little squeeze. She flinched at the gesture but gave me a small smile before pulling away.

"Avah," a familiar voice said. I turned as Kat reached me and sat down beside me. Her beauty still stunned me. How could anyone be this elegant, this perfect?

"Kat—umm, Milady, hello."

She brushed off my fumble. "Please, call me Kat. I've never been one for formalities." She glanced from me to Malik and then back again so quickly I wondered if I'd just imagined it.

"Thank you... Kat." Her casualness was uncomfortable. When it was time to discuss business, we referred to Amicia with her title. The same happened with my former witch coven. I had never met someone who held so much power and didn't want to remind you of said power every chance they got. I also found it incredibly amusing that Malik, of all vampires, was falling into the forbidden love. I smiled on the inside at the thought.

"I've been very worried. Jasik wouldn't let anyone see you. Not even me." Her lips pursed.

"He's protective," I said, and his hand squeezed my thigh under the table.

"For good measure," Sebastian said. "Or do I need to remind you that she nearly *died*."

Malik tensed, his fist slamming against the table in a moment of weakness. I don't know what surprised me more: Sebastian's blatant disrespect for an elder or Malik's impulsive protectiveness for his *lady friend*.

"Relax, big boy, you're no match," Sebastian said, brushing

off Malik's aggressive behavior. "I've seen death, more times than I can count. I've never seen someone survive on the brink like that. Without a doubt, Avah should have died yesterday. The fact that she's here is a miracle."

I gasped and looked at Sebastian. "It was that bad?" I whispered.

He nodded slowly and looked away. Jasik tensed beside me.

"I knew it was bad, but… I didn't realize… Do you think it was that witch? Maybe she did something?"

Sebastian shrugged. "Doubtful. What is one fire witch going to do? She'd need a complete elemental set, and I doubt *that* happened."

I nodded. He was right. "I guess my *destiny* hasn't been fulfilled yet. Someone up there needs me down here." I tried to lighten the mood, but it didn't work. We were too tense, too raw.

"In any event, I'm happy you're here. I want you to understand that. You are always welcome here." Kat smiled brightly at me.

"Oh, um, thanks. It's been nice staying here. Albeit weird. But nice."

"Weird? How so?"

"I just… I'm ready to be home." I felt Jasik's hand squeeze, and I looked up at him. He smiled at me, no doubt loving that I referred to the manor as *home*.

"Of course. It's only natural to be where your heart is.

Perhaps, eventually, you'll open your heart to us, too. We'd love for you to all visit again soon."

I couldn't deny her hidden meaning. She wanted me to feel comfortable here, because Jasik followed wherever I went, and Malik followed him. We were a team, and she wanted this team to return often.

"Definitely. Maybe we could even have our own bedrooms," I said with a wink.

"Yes, of course! If that would make you more comfortable, I'll see to that." She beamed, and I felt bad, as if I was leading her on to believe we'd stay here permanently. I wasn't sure how this worked, but Jasik and Malik were sired by Amicia. I was sure they needed to stay as her Hunters.

"Oh, I didn't mean that seriously. I was kidding. The guest rooms are fine."

She nodded, looking lost for words.

"We were actually going to start a locater spell before we head out," I said, hoping to relieve the awkwardness of Malik shifting around, Kat staring at the table, and Sebastian giving his alpha glares at the vampires around the room.

"Very good. You'll let me know if you need anything from me, yes?" I nodded. "Well, then. Until we meet again, Avah." She grasped my free hand, and a look of longing flashed before her eyes. She dropped my hand and faced Malik. "I need to speak with you before you go." And with that, she left us in silence.

I slurped down my mugs of blood.

"Well, this is awkward," Jeremiah said, looking from vampire to vampire.

Malik stood abruptly, his chair scratching against the floor in an ear-piercing cry. "Do you need me for the spell?"

"Nope," I said with a grin.

"Avah, please." He shook his head as he left us and reunited with his lover.

"Am I really the only one who's going to acknowledge this?" I asked. Lillie immediately began playing with her mug, sliding it from hand to hand. Jeremiah's eyebrows waggled, and I groaned in response. Jasik squeezed my hand and shook his head. Sebastian arched an eyebrow and bit his lower lip. "They're clearly sleeping together. What's so bad about that?"

"This isn't up for discussion," Jasik said sharply. His harsh tone made me jerk as if he'd just lashed me. He'd never spoken to me with his authoritative voice, and I wasn't sure I liked it... at all.

"Always so eager to protect your brother?" Sebastian asked.

"Always eager to protect what's *mine*."

I gawked as anger seemed to seep from Jasik's pores. "Okay, what happened while I was knocked out?"

"You mean while you were *dying*?" Jasik asked, and I cowered. His tone was bitter, though I knew he didn't mean it to be.

"Ouch." I pried my hand from his grip. "Harsh much?"

"I'm sorry. I didn't mean—" He ran a hand through his messy hair.

"Forget it. I just don't see the issue here," I said.

"Too much has happened. We're all on edge."

I nodded, waiting for him to continue as I watched his eyes cloud over.

"You almost died, Amicia is missing, and Kat…" He shook his head.

"What about Kat?"

"She wants us to relinquish our duties to Amicia and join her coven." He spoke softly, as if it hurt him to say the words aloud.

"What? Are you kidding? Can that even happen?"

"We're bound to Amicia in more ways than one," he said simply.

"Okay? Meaning?"

"Malik will not leave unless I leave, and it's not as simple for me. Amicia is our sire. I've never imagined walking away from her."

"But the woman he loves is here, so he has to choose between her and you." I said what he wouldn't.

"Yes," he whispered. "My bond to my brother is stronger than my bond to Amicia, and if it were you, I'd leave without a second thought. But… it's just not that simple." His eyes were painful, murky puddles of blue. Their usual life, their usual flare, was gone. It pained him to make this decision, and he knew he'd have to. Malik wouldn't leave him, but would he resent him?

"I'll go wherever you go, Jasik. I need you to know that." I rested my hand against his thigh.

He smiled, trailing his fingers against my cheek before tucking my hair behind my ear. *I love you so much, Avah.*

I bit my lip. "I love you, too."

He tensed beside me. "What?"

I frowned. What was the issue? We'd admitted our love for each other in front of others more times than I could count.

"What did you say?"

"I said I love you, too…" I glanced at the others, who shared equally puzzled looks as they met my eyes. Except for Sebastian and Lillie. They gave me knowing glances.

"I didn't say that aloud. I *thought* that."

"You did? I didn't—I didn't even notice. It was so loud, so clear. I thought you just… said it." I glanced at Sebastian.

"That's how it is," Lillie said. I met her gaze. "When you've gotten control, it's like that. It's actually kinda hard to intentionally separate the two. It took me years to stop answering someone's thoughts."

I smiled and shrieked in delight. "Finally!" I screamed. We weren't alone in the dining hall. I could feel eyes on my back, but I didn't care. "Finally! I've been *dying* to get some control! I thought I'd only get control of healing, which I can't even really take credit for. It just *happens.*"

"Your abilities should be mindless, Avah. That's the point. In the beginning, you'll work for them, but eventually, they'll happen as naturally as blinking. Your powers *are* you, not an extension of you."

I nodded with a cheeky grin. "I'll admit, I didn't really hear everything you just said, because I can't stop listening to your inner thoughts!" I shrieked, unable to control my laughter. "This is going to be great!"

Sebastian rolled his eyes. "Relax, killer, or I'll block you."

"I've never heard your thoughts," Lillie said with a pout, crossing her arms over her chest.

"That's a good thing, pet. You wouldn't want to hear the dirty things I think about." His gaze darkened as he leaned toward her. He licked his lips, and she shuddered under his gaze.

"This will be interesting," Jasik said. "I've never had relations with a reader."

"Guess now's the time to let me know all those secrets you've been keeping." I winked.

"From you, I keep nothing." He placed a kiss on the top of my head as he stood. "We should get started."

My excitement quickly dwindled as I thought about the task at hand. With the help of the hybrids, the locater spell would be easy work. I had no doubt that we'd find Amicia's location today. I was more concerned about tapping into the vision I'd had with Sebastian. I'd have to tell them what I'd seen, but first, I needed to know more.

CHAPTER
THIRTEEN

Sebastian and I sat alone in the woods, though the others were lurking nearby. They'd come running to both protect and lend us power. We had already used the sage stick to smudge our impurities away before entering the crystal circle. We were facing each other, cross-legged. The familiar tug of magic warmed me, and I wondered if Sebastian felt the same pull. I knew he missed this. He'd admitted that the first time we'd done magic together.

"Ready, sugar?" he asked breathlessly.

I nodded, the weight of magic already sitting heavily upon me.

Together, we bit into our wrists, and before our magic could heal the wound, we slapped them together. I gripped his hand as his blood coursed through me. The crystals surrounding our circle glowed brightly—a sign that we were tapped into our magic. I swayed back and forth, relishing the feeling of Sebastian's power as it seeped into me. He was so strong, so undeniably strong. Underneath his sweet-talking ways, a dangerous, powerful predator lurked. The air tingled around us, and our surroundings began to fade away as our blood magic once again took control.

I no longer felt the cool, brisk air dance across my skin. I no longer saw the trees or looming manor. I no longer heard the snap of twigs under a hybrid's feet. I no longer felt Jasik's lurking essence.

There was only Sebastian, and there was only me.

A light mist coated our skin and dripped down the curve of my bare back. I wore my signature hunting outfit: sports bra and shorts. This was the first outfit I was given when Amicia took me in, and it felt right to find her while wearing it.

"*Spiritum Spiritu voccat te. Spiritu Spiritus indicaret mihi*," I whispered, calling to the spirit power within Sebastian and me and begging it to connect with Amicia's essence. "*Spiritum Spiritu voccat te. Spiritu Spiritus indicaret mihi*," I said again, this time more forcefully.

A wave of magic hit me, nearly separating my connection to Sebastian as I connected with Amicia.

My body swayed as I fought to stop myself from toppling over. Sebastian's hand reached out, steadying me.

Once again, I saw only the flash of images Amicia had seen.

"Stay focused," he said. "Ignore the past. Find the present." Sebastian's voice was calm, soft. He radiated around me.

I nodded, my head heavy. I fought the urge to rest against Sebastian.

The army of Rogues flashed before my eyes, and I bit my lip in an attempt to control my fear. They surrounded me. I could hear them, see them, smell them. It was as if they stood before me now. I jerked as one reached his hand forward and met skin— Amicia's skin. He struck her. She didn't cry out.

"Shield your thoughts, Avah," he said, and I obeyed, quickly drawing upon my shield, strengthening its hold on my mind. I didn't need the others seeing what I saw—especially not when I had plans to reach deeper into my visions.

I cringed at the sight of them. "There are so many. So many Rogues. Hundreds…"

No one spoke. No one wanted to admit the truth: we were severely outnumbered. The likelihood that we'd survive was slim.

"Span out. See more," Sebastian urged.

"I see… trees. A lot of trees. It's remote, very rural. Very cold." I was breathless. My arm ached, and my stomach grumbled. I was growing weaker by the minute. The wind shifted around me, and someone grasped my arm in a tight squeeze. I glanced up under heavy eyes. The hybrid's hand squeezed me tightly, and I felt him shift as another latched on, lending his power, too. The power rush surged through me, seeping into my pores.

"What else?" he asked, and I closed my eyes again.

"She's really close. Closer than she was before. We're going the right way."

"Good. Anything else? Look for a sign. Look for anything that tells us where to look." Sebastian's voice was louder, stronger as another hybrid joined our circle.

A sign. Something. Anything. I willed myself to find a clue—a necessary clue. The one that would lead us to her.

"I need more!" I cried out. The wind shifted as one by one, more hybrids joined our circle. I inhaled sharply, the power almost too much to contain.

"Find something, Avah. You can do it. Believe you can. Force the magic to do your bidding," Sebastian said.

I nodded, searching the trees. I came upon endless dirt roads, waterfalls and creaks, mountains, black bears and moose, snowy trees, and... "I think... Alaska?" I prayed I was right. I had never been there, but I had watched television, and I was pretty sure the only place we'd find that remote setting with black bears and moose was in Alaska.

"Good! Where?" Sebastian asked, attempting to guide me to

an exact location.

I shook my head. "I—I can't tell."

"Span out. Stay focused."

I pulled away, feeling as if my essence was coasting over land, flying in the sky. It was only a high from the blood magic, but everything felt so real. I was sure if I reached out, I could touch the trees. I followed the road, hoping it'd lead me to a building. Instead, it twisted and winded along dirt paths with no end in sight. I blinked and came across a dirt-covered jeep. It looked abandoned, with a broken windshield and flat tires.

"I see... a car, a jeep."

"Look at the plate," Sebastian ordered. "What does it say?"

I reached forward in an attempt to brush away the debris, but my arm fell limp.

"You can't touch it, Avah. You're not really there. What can you see?"

I shook my head slowly. "Nothing. A couple letters, a yellow plate."

My breathing became heavy; the vision was slipping. It felt as if something was pulling me back, as if I'd gotten too close. In a flash, two red irises were staring at me. I jumped back and screamed as the Rogue's nose brushed against mine. I felt it outside of the vision, as if the monster was standing before me.

"That's enough. We've seen everything we need to see. It's

time to withdraw," Sibyl said. I felt her step within the circle and reach my side.

"No! Not yet," I argued, keeping my hold on the line of hybrids, who fell to their knees before me as I drained them.

"Stop!" Sibyl yelled. Her shield enveloped her hybrids, breaking our connection.

"No!" I screamed. I dropped my arm, defeated. We may have seen enough to figure out where Amicia is, but I still hadn't tapped into my earlier visions. Something was coming for us, and we weren't going to survive. I *needed* to see more. I had to stop it. I just needed a few more minutes...

Sibyl squatted beside me. "You're stronger than you realize, Avah. You could have killed them. I won't risk even one of mine for an outsider."

I grabbed onto her hand, grasping it tightly as I yanked her to the ground. I screamed as I forced my shield from me too quickly; it rippled from in waves, knocking back anything in its path.

"Avah! What are you doing?" Sebastian yelled from beyond my shield.

"*Spiritus dicam tibi. Educite illam potentiam, do mihi. Spiritus dicam tibi. Educite illam potentiam, do mihi,*" I called, stealing Sibyl's power and transferring it to me.

I was transported back into my vision, pulling strength from

Sibyl. She was the most powerful hybrid I'd ever encountered. Her power would be enough. She screamed as I drained her of her essence. Her skin aged before my eyes, her flesh sunken, clinging to her bones in a pathetic attempt at maintaining life. Her cries echoed in my mind, but I pushed them aside. I just needed a few minutes. Just enough to see who was targeting us. I had to believe Sibyl would understand. She'd do the same thing to save her people.

Our magic catapulted into me, and I was transported to another time. The world around me became hazy, leaving altogether.

Thump. Thump. Thump. My heart pounded in my head. It was so loud, too loud. I couldn't concentrate on anything but the strong, steady beat of my heart.

"H—Hello?" I called, moving my arms around the darkness that consumed me. Slowly, the haze began to clear, and I could open my eyes. I brought my arms up to shield my eyes, the light in the room blinding. My senses adjusted.

The room was illuminated by a dim bedside lamp. I looked around. I knew the room well. I was back at the manor, in the secret hospital room. I lifted my arms, but there was nothing there—no IVs. I sat up, grunting as I wobbled off the cot.

"Hello? Jasik?"

I stumbled to the door and yanked it open. The hall outside my room was dark. I leaned against the wall and stalked toward the stairs, crawling up them on my hands and knees. I was tired, weak, my legs too heavy. I pulled myself into the foyer, and standing, I stumbled out the front door.

I saw them.

Jasik, Malik, Jeremiah, Lillie, Amicia, the vampires of the manor, witches from my coven, and the hybrids... they were dead. All dead. Some lay in pieces. Others were slit open from neck to navel. I screamed, rushing toward them, and toppled over, tripping. I glanced over and found Sebastian staring back at me, his eyes lifeless, his neck ripped open. I cried out, reaching for him. A chuckle distracted me, and I sat up too quickly. Red irises stared at me from the distance as I cowered in the corner. There were hundreds staring back at me; they glowed against the darkness of the night. I swallowed hard, willing myself to remember that this was a vision, that I wasn't really there. I felt a tug on my arm and looked down, watching Sibyl as she took her last breath. Her lifeless body stared up at me, her hand falling limp in mine.

"Sibyl!"

I dropped her hand, breaking our connection. I toppled over, and my shield fell. The hybrids pounced into action. Those who didn't retrieve Sibyl's frail body were on me. Hands grasped my throat, lifting me off the ground. I stared into furious violet irises, and I knew they would end me... for her.

I released my shield. It slammed into the hybrids, flinging their bodies back, and I collapsed to the ground. Before I hit, I was in Jasik's arms. I was too weak to maintain my shield. He set me down gently and stood. My head lolled over, and I found Jasik, Malik, Lillie, Jeremiah, and Sebastian standing before me, separating the hybrids from me.

"She didn't mean to hurt her," Jasik began. "She did it for our priestess. You can relate to taking extreme measures to save your own, I'm sure."

"I don't care! She went too far," someone yelled.

"Sibyl's strong. She'll be fine once she feeds," Sebastian offered.

"It's still unacceptable. Avah can't be trusted!" someone else yelled.

My eyes were heavy, and I knew I'd drift into unconsciousness if I didn't feed soon.

"Stop!" I heard Sibyl yell, her voice weak. "Let her go."

The Hunters separated as Sibyl approached me, dropping to her knees before offering me her dripping wrist.

I ignored the gasps as I drank from her, my eyes never leaving hers. I didn't need much. Her blood coursed through my system within seconds of entering my mouth. It rejuvenated me. I released her, feeling stronger than I'd ever felt. I frowned at her as I sat up, still unsure why she'd help me after I betrayed her trust so hastily. I hadn't even second-guessed my decision. I knew I was doing the right thing—even if that meant taking her life.

Avah. Her voice filled my head, and I recoiled instinctively at the intrusion. *I saw everything.*

⸙

"We tell no one," Sibyl said as we padded through the forest, miles away from the manor. It had been a fight to allow me to go alone with her. Jasik, the Hunters, and Sebastian weren't too keen on the idea. They thought she'd kill me as soon as I was away from my protectors. Finally, they seemed to remember that I alone took her down, so they agreed. But they made it known that if I wasn't back in twenty minutes, they'd come looking.

"Are you sure that's the best idea?" I understood her concern. I'd experienced the same emotions with my former witch coven. She wanted to protect her hybrids just as much as I had wanted to protect my witches. "Last time I hid something like this, it didn't go well."

I thought back to the night I'd first encountered the Hunters. They let me live, and I refused to tell my coven of the attack. That night, Rogues found us, killing many. I died that night, and though I believed I was now living my true destiny—and not some messed up version the witches had in mind—I still wondered how that night would have played out differently if I didn't keep the secret, if I just would have told them.

"Or perhaps you're looking at it the wrong way. Maybe things went exactly how they were supposed to go." She arched her eyebrows as I looked at her. Her shoulder-length hair was wildly curly, and her violet irises glowed against the dark brown mane.

"I just don't want to make a mistake," I said.

She stopped abruptly and faced me. "Again, Avah, you're looking at this negatively. You need to stop looking at your new life as a mistake. It will only hold you back." Her thick accent coated her sincere words.

I nodded. "I know. Jasik believes that, too. He thinks we were meant to be together." I gazed up at her, trying to read her expression, but she gave me nothing. I knew she didn't like the idea of a hybrid with a Hunter just as much as Sebastian hated the idea of a vampire working with a witch. They held onto a grudge that didn't need to exist.

"I see." She turned on her heel and began walking back toward the manor. I was sure our twenty minutes would soon be up.

"So we just let everyone die? Including us?"

She smiled. "No, my dear, we don't. You're forgetting that a seer's ability was created with the intention of *changing* the future, not simply to see it. Now that we know what's coming, we'll be prepared."

"But they won't," I argued.

"They will, because we will. Knowing this information has already changed our course. Time is complicated that way. Because we know, we've already changed it. It's already been done. The motions are in place. We just need to see them through."

I kicked the frosted ground at my feet. "So… we tell no one."

"Not yet. First, we fight, we find Amicia, we survive this battle. We can worry about this problem then."

I nodded.

"We need everyone to think clearly. No one can do that when they're on their deathbed."

"So for *now*, we tell no one."

She didn't speak. She didn't need to. We both knew it would play out this way. She wanted to protect her hybrids, and I wanted to protect my new family. There wasn't anything she or I wouldn't do to see that through.

∽

I stalked into the dining hall, anxious to refuel before we made the journey to Alaska. As usual, the hall was packed with vampires.

My eyes scanned the room in search of Jasik, and I stopped in my tracks. In the far corner, four sets of glowing eyes were on me, but they weren't the glowing eyes I'd seen day in and day out. The Hunters of this house had returned from their trip, and I could see their hesitation. They weren't sure if I was friend or foe, which only put me on guard.

"Avah!" a voice called, and I pried my eyes away, looking in the sound's direction. I found Jasik smiling at me from his usual spot in the corner. A lone chair sat beside him, and I took it.

"Sleep well?" Jasik asked, and I nodded.

"Where's Sebastian?" I glanced around, needing to see a friendly and familiar set of violet irises.

"Outside. Thought it was best to not be here today," Jeremiah said as he glanced at the other Hunters.

"Mmm," I mumbled. "Probably smart."

"You feel it, too?" Lillie asked.

I met her gaze. "Feel what?" I attempted innocence, but inside, I was grateful that it wasn't just me who questioned them.

"They want us gone," she answered.

I nodded. "Makes sense, I suppose."

"How so?" Jeremiah asked, and Jasik tensed beside me. I was known for my bluntness, and even with Malik quietly sipping his breakfast, I'd say what everyone else thought.

"Kat hasn't exactly been quiet about her intentions. She wants us, which means she doesn't want them."

A chair scraped against the ground harshly, the metal bringing an ear-piercing squeak to my sensitive ears. I shuddered and glanced over my shoulder. They stood and left, but never did their angry gazes leave mine until they were past the door. I shook my head as I sat back in my chair, slurping down a mug of blood.

"We have more important things to discuss," Malik said, and I shrugged. We did, but this was also important. Soon, we'd find her, go home, and then we'd need to stop hiding the elephant in the room. I hoped they'd come to that understanding themselves—without any prying from me. The last thing I wanted to do was spend an eternity with a pissed off Malik.

"Right," Jasik said as he leaned forward and pulled a passport from the back pocket of his dark jeans. Only then did I realize the others weren't in their usual, risqué attire. Only I bared skin. They were in jeans, shirts, and coats. They almost looked… human.

"What's with the clothes?" I asked.

"I set something on the bed for you. Did you not see it?"

I shook my head. "Guess I didn't." In truth, I had seen it, but I thought he was kidding. He always encouraged me to be comfortable in my skin and the nearly sky-clad attire we had to wear when hunting. I should have known he was serious—he

194

really wasn't one to joke.

"Well, you'll need to change. You stick out in that." His gaze slid down my practically nude frame, and I felt my cheeks flush.

"Calm down," Jeremiah said with a catcall.

I rolled my eyes.

"We've got tickets to take the ferry from Bellingham to Ketchikan. Ketchikan is at the base of Tongass, a 17-million-acre national forest. Based on your vision, they're not near human population, and with a little research, we thought we'd start there. We can span out, cover more ground."

I nodded. "Sounds like a good plan to me. Plus, once we're closer, maybe Sebastian and I can try again."

"No." Jasik's no nonsense tone bared its ugly head.

"We got further this last time. I saw more—"

"You also almost died."

"Well, not because of the magic."

"Exactly. You weren't thinking clearly. I understand your motives, but your actions almost got everyone killed. It's a miracle Sibyl forgave you. I was sure there'd be a fight."

I shuddered and grasped his hand, which sat casually atop the table. "I didn't… I didn't think about that. I'm sorry." I looked at the others. "I'd never do something that'd get you hurt. You have to know that."

Jeremiah smiled and placed his hand over mine and Jasik's. "Of course not. We know that."

Jasik cleared his throat and pulled his hand away. I couldn't deny the cold shiver that shot down my spine as I grasped my mug. I knew he was upset with me, with my actions, but I also knew he understood how important they were. He thought it was all for Amicia. I hated keeping this secret from him, and I wasn't sure I was strong enough to keep lying—especially if I'd be getting the cold shoulder. I needed Jasik and I to be on the same level.

"I got you a passport. We may need it to get off the ferry in Alaska since it technically makes stops in Canada, too. I'm not sure, so I got one just in case." He passed it to me with a shaky hand. I frowned at it and looked up at him. His eyes were cloudy, unsure. I'd never seen Jasik lose his confident demeanor, his alpha glare. Was he really *that* upset with me? He couldn't even look at me?

I gave him a weak smile and said, "Thank you." I grabbed the passport and opened it. A vast array of emotions came over me: confusion, denial, comfort, longing… I stared into my former chocolate brown eyes. My long, dark hair sat in perfect waves around my shoulders, and my makeup was neatly made in a natural style. I could see just the tops of my black sweater. A silver chain hung from my neck. Though I could only see a corner of the chain, I knew a small cross was just out of the camera's sight;

it rested just below my collar bones. I remembered the day as if it'd just happened yesterday. This photo was taken in my last year of college. I was nervous when I took my student ID photo, but not because everyone tended to get *awful* pictures. I was nervous because this was the last year I'd have to myself. The girl in the photo still thought she was a chosen one and would soon give her life for the cause. I'd had no idea what future awaited me once I graduated…

I glanced up and found Jasik staring at me. His look was controlled, but there was something else there, a mixture of fear and longing. I'd seen that same look on my passport photo. I wondered how long it'd take for him to get over what I'd done to Sibyl. In all honesty, I thought he was being a bit dramatic.

"How did you get this made so quickly?" I asked, hoping to smooth things over.

He swallowed. "We have connections. I made the trip while you were in town with Sebastian. The picture… it's from—"

"My college ID. I know." I gave him a puzzled looking, hoping I wouldn't have to ask just how he'd gotten it.

"Ever met a techie vampire, Avah?" Jeremiah said with a grin.

"Can't say I have," I answered.

"Eh, it's probably better that way. They're a double threat in my opinion. They can hack into computers *and* hearts." Jeremiah laughed loudly at his joke, and I laughed at him. It didn't matter if our world was falling apart; the optimist in him always loved life and would make the best of any situation.

I glanced back down at the passport, my eyes scanning the details. I stopped short on my name: *Avah Lavery.*

"Avah Lavery?"

Jasik inhaled sharply, and I arched my eyebrow at him. He was acting *weird.*

"Well, I guess I can't be Avah Taylor forever, right? Where'd Lavery come from?" His irises glowed bright neon blue as he searched my eyes.

"That's my name," Jasik said softly. "Jasik Lavery."

My eyes widened as the realization hit me hard. I understood his longing, his fear. In all his years—all seven hundred or so years—he'd likely never given a woman his name. I was the first, and I promised myself I'd be the last. I smiled and leaned forward, pressing my lips against his. Under my touch, he softened. I understood. His weird behavior wasn't really because of what I'd done to Sibyl. It was because he planned to offer me something that he couldn't take back if my reaction went south. The meaning behind the passport affected more than his mood: it affected our future as a couple.

"I like it," I whispered, pretending the others weren't awkwardly staring at us. "Avah Lavery." I bit my lip.

Malik cleared his throat. "It's safer to travel as a family. We won't draw as much attention."

I ignored Malik and his attempt to brush off this serious step forward in my relationship with Jasik. What he'd done was as good as a proposal in my book. I didn't need the fancy words, expensive jewelry, or the exotic locations. I just needed to know that he was *mine* and I was *his*.

"It's a two day trip from Bellingham to Ketchikan, and we'll need to stay off top deck," Malik continued.

I nodded, but I wasn't really listening. I was sure I had a goofy grin on my face, but all that mattered was that Jasik's look matched mine.

FOURTEEN

The two days on board the ferry went by quickly. The Hunters, Sebastian, and I stayed on the lower decks, wearing colored contacts and sunglasses. I wasn't sure if I'd be able survive being completed surrounded by humans—especially going without food for more than a day—but I was able to control my hunger well enough. When I couldn't, I fed from Jasik, an excruciatingly erotic experience when you had to share a room with four others. Our room slept six, and while I was happy to keep the Hunters and Sebastian close, I couldn't ignore the anxiety I felt whenever I wondered where the hybrids were. To get on and off the ferry, I had to show a form of ID, so I was grateful for the passport. Every time I saw it, I smiled, and more times than not, I found Jasik gazing at me lovingly when I did so.

Now, I sunk to the ground, licking my fingers. Before me, the hybrids and Hunters messily slurped the last drops of the wild animals we'd hunted for food. We hadn't eaten in two days, and though we weren't necessarily weak because of it, we were nervous about our impending Rogue encounter. We weren't kidding ourselves: It usually took four well-trained Hunters to take down one weak Rogue. We decided refueling, *just in case*, was the best option. I still wore the skin-tight black leggings, sports bra, and over-sized sweater that Jasik insisted I wear aboard the ferry. The others hadn't changed, either, and I figured they wouldn't. Once we got Amicia, we'd need to blend again, so there was no point in changing. I hadn't mentioned our lack of weapons. I was used to fighting with blades, though my strength and abilities would make me just as lethal of a killer without them. I silently thanked Sebastian for teaching me to semi-control my powers, and briefly, I wondered if he'd known all along that I wouldn't have my trusty seax with me during battle.

"We should regroup," Malik said, and Jasik nodded in return.

A high-pitched whistle pierced my ears, and I squinted at the sound.

"Jeremiah! Way to announce our location to *everyone*, you idiot!" Lillie scolded. Jeremiah's face fell at the realization.

I shrugged. "Chances are, they know we're here." I offered

him a reassuring smile, though I doubted it helped him feel better.

The hybrids circled us, and Jasik began hashing out details. "We'll span out in teams. At least one hybrid with one Hunter at all times. Once we find her, we'll signal to others, spreading the word. We want to avoid confrontation until we have Amicia, if at all possible."

The Hunters nodded in unison.

"I'll pair with Sebastian, Avah with Malik, Sibyl with Lillie and Jeremiah, and…"

Jasik had planned for us to stay in smaller groups while we scoped the 17 million acres. Once we'd found them, the news would spread like wildfire until we all met up again at the location. No one argued as we began to separate, so I assumed it was as good a plan as any. I gave Sebastian, Lillie, and Jeremiah the strongest bear-hugs I could muster, while whispering sweet nothings into their ears like "be careful," "watch your back," and "please don't die." They hugged me back and offered the same phrases. I turned to Jasik, and he scooped me up in his arms. My legs wrapped around his waist as his mouth crashed down on mine. His kiss was hungry, greedy, and passionate. He kissed me as if he'd never get the chance again. When we finally broke apart, nearly everyone had left.

"I've paired you with Malik. You're the two most important people in my life. Don't be reckless, Avah, please."

I smiled at him and placed a soft kiss on his forehead. "Never."

"Malik will keep you safe," he said, his gaze lingering on Malik.

"As if she were my own," Malik responded, bringing his arm across his chest in a close-fisted salute.

"And I'll keep him safe," I said, meeting Malik's gaze. He nodded once and turned to give us privacy.

"I love you, Avah," he whispered, his lips grazing my temple as I rested my head against him. "More than you'll ever know."

I closed my eyes, and for just a moment, I pretended all was right with the world. We weren't in a race against time. We weren't attempting the unachievable. We weren't staring at death's door. We were just us... Avah and Jasik. Two crazy kids who fell in love and wanted to spend the rest of their lives together.

And then I opened my eyes, and reality sank in.

Jasik lowered me as I said, "I love you, too, Mr. Lavery." I gave him a knowing wink. I stood on my heels, and he leaned down to meet me. I bypassed his kiss and brushed my lips against his ear. "And before this war is over, I'm going to marry you."

He inhaled sharply, his head turning to meet my gaze. His eyes were two neon shades of burning blue, and they betrayed his hope, his love... both, for me.

My feet pounded against the frozen tundra that was rural southern Alaska. I struggled to keep up with Malik as he pushed forward, silently searching for signs of life. We saw no Rogue footprints, no broken twigs, nothing. I was beginning to believe we'd chosen the wrong direction when he came to an abrupt stop.

"What is it?" I whispered.

He shook his head. "Nothing. Bear track."

I exhaled quickly. Glancing around, I took in our surroundings. I could hear the steady stream of a creek in the distance. The tall, thick hemlock and spruce towered over us, seemingly rising for miles and miles. The forest was dense, providing much needed covering, though I doubted Rogues were lurking nearby. A fresh layer of soft snow coated the twigs that snapped under our weight.

"I heard what you said," Malik said as he brushed his fingers across the stump of a tree. The branches stuck out at awkward angles, indicating something had come past. Was it the bear? Or could it have been something else?

"Oh?" I said, playing it cool. Clearly, I was an expert at nonchalant.

"He will, you know." He kept his gaze downward, as if the branches he inspected would jump forward with information at any moment.

"What?" I focused on the knot that formed in my throat.

"Marry you."

I swallowed, ignoring the giddy feeling that clouded my mind whenever I thought about Jasik and I together… forever.

"He's different with you."

"You're different with Kat," I countered.

He stiffened.

"Seriously? What's the big deal?" I had never seen adults act like such children over mutual feelings.

He turned abruptly to face me. His hands were in tight fists at his sides, and anger fumed from him. I flinched as if he'd hit me. He must've noticed, because he softened quickly. "I don't expect you to understand."

"Why? Because I'm an *outsider*?" I used dramatic air quotes to make my point. "Because Jasik broke some ridiculous vampire law when he changed me? Because—"

"Because that's not *him*. Jasik would never put himself or us in danger, and that's what he did *for* you. He put you above all else—him, us, me…"

"And that's why you hate me?"

He scoffed. "I don't *hate* you, Avah."

"Well, you're pretty damn good at making everyone else think you hate me."

"That's your impression and nothing more. This is me. I

don't have time for games or ridiculous high school emotions. Every day, I fight to survive. Every day, I throw myself in front of danger because it is my duty. And every day I survive an attack, I remind myself that *that's* what's important. *That's* why I've survived as long as I have. Jasik did the same. For nearly seven hundred years, we walked side by side, with nothing to come between us… until you."

I released the breath I had been choking on. "Malik," I whispered as I eliminated the space between us. I pulled him down into a tight embrace, resting my head in the curve of his neck. He stiffened at the show of affection, and I found myself believing he really had been so closed off for as many years as he recounted. "No one will ever replace you in Jasik's eyes. You're his flesh and blood. You're his brother. You're the most important person in his life. He would die for you, kill for you."

Malik pulled away, his eyes hard. "You mean more to him than you realize."

"I could say the same," I countered.

He tried to brush away my admission with the wave of his hand. I was elated that he was finally opening up—to *me* of all people—and I couldn't let him close himself off again, not when happiness was at stake.

"Malik, don't you see? He'll leave *her* for you."

His eyes met mine, and I knew he understood. Jasik had been bound to Amicia for nearly a thousand years. She meant everything to him. She offered them an eternity when they had but minutes to live. She was their sire, and that bonded them. But he would walk away... for him. For Malik. For Malik's love for Kat.

"You love her, and Jasik sees that. When we return, he'll tell Amicia, and we'll leave. He'll do that. For you. For your chance at an eternal love. He'll do that, even though it goes against everything he knows to be right, so you can have a chance *with her.*"

He swallowed hard but said nothing. The walls he forced back up were slowly crumbling again.

"Nothing will ever be easy for us, Malik. We're undead vampires, for Christ's sake! But our love for each other will always come naturally. You mean something to him, and you mean something to me. You're more than a friend or a fellow Hunter or a roommate who has emotional issues." His eyes narrowed, but I continued. "You're a brother. You're *my* brother. Maybe not by blood, but by faith, by loyalty. And I will never stand between you and yours."

He nodded, and then in a moment of weakness, he yanked me back to him, pulling me into a tight embrace. "I can see why he loves you."

"'Cause I'm totally easy to love." I grinned as I felt the tightness in Malik's body finally lift. "Life is going to be hard, but loving each other will never be difficult. Not unless we let it."

I pulled away as he pressed a kiss to my forehead. I closed my eyes, enjoying the feeling of his lingering lips. I had no sexual feelings for Malik—even though it could be argued that he was Jasik's doppelgänger. It was obvious they were brothers. In fact, very few physical differences set them apart. To the average onlooker, it'd be easy to fall for either. But I never had that issue. When we first met, and from every moment onward, I only saw Jasik. I only *ever* saw Jasik.

"What?" he asked, puzzled, though a sly smile began to form. It might take him a century, but at some point, he'd realize that I'd meant more to him than he ever realized. But I planned to let him figure that out himself.

"You've shown me more emotion in the past five minutes than you've shown me in the last month! Wait... Scratch that. This whole trip has been like an episode of *The Twilight Zone*. What's up with you?" I gave him a playful smile and winked.

He rolled his eyes and started to walk away.

"Did you just roll your eyes at me? That's another emotion, Malik," I said sarcastically.

He scoffed, stomping through the brush, eager to leave me behind. But when he thought I wasn't looking, I caught the remnants of a smile he'd been trying to hide.

CHAPTER
FIFTEEN

"I can feel her," Malik whispered. We'd been walking around the woods for hours. We had run into a few other hybrids and promptly searched a new direction. There was no time for pleasantries. We were getting antsy and wondering if we'd chosen the wrong part of Alaska.

I closed my eyes, trying to sense her, but came up blank.

"You weren't sired by her, Avah. You won't feel the pull as naturally as I do." I opened my eyes and found him staring at me.

"Oh."

"Let's keep moving. She's near." He was quick to change subjects, but his lingering emotion was there, in his eyes. He liked that I tried to sense her the way he could. He liked that I searched for that same connection.

I stalked behind him, staying as alert as possible and silently wishing I had my seax. We came to a clearing that broke off several yards in front of us. Malik hesitated while I sauntered closer, staying quick and quiet on my feet. When I reached the edge of the cliff, I glanced down and stumbled backward. Before I hit the ground, Malik was behind me. He pulled me up, and I rested against his frame, shaking.

"What—"

I reached forward in a flash, pushing my hand against his mouth. With wide eyes, I shook my head. When I removed my hand, I pointed down the cliff.

Rogues, I mouthed.

He released me and sidestepped so he could look down. His face hardened when he'd seen what I'd seen.

There were hundreds, maybe thousands. They sat, they talked, they rested, they ate, they killed. There were small huts, which I found interesting. How long had they been here? Their numbers were impressive, so I assumed this had been in the works long before I joined the vampire ranks. Even so, I found myself wondering: Why? How? When? Rogues weren't smart creatures. They lived for the blood, the kill. They didn't think things through. They were erratic and impulsive. But someone had to be leading them, keeping them in their place while plans were drawn.

I shivered at the thought of someone powerful enough to control this many Rogues.

This secret society of Rogues had my head spinning and gut wrenching. Malik stepped back, scooped me up, and ran. It may have been a bit dramatic on his part since I didn't need the lift, but I closed my eyes and sank against him, inviting the comfort. When he stopped abruptly, I heard him bark out orders before he set me down.

"Avah?" a familiar voice asked.

I turned to find Sebastian and Jasik behind me.

"We... found them." I closed my eyes, clearly pictured what I'd seen, and temporarily lowered my shield. My eyes shot open as Sebastian exhaled sharply. His hand was to his mouth, and his fear was plastered across his face. Jasik's worry matched Sebastian's as I explained what Malik and I encountered.

"Holy fuck," Sebastian said. "We're seriously outnumbered."

"Doesn't matter," Sibyl said as she snuck up on us. I spun around and faced her. "They are a threat we cannot ignore."

"So we charge full throttle and get killed? Perfect plan!" Sebastian said, arms flailing.

"No, we calculate each attack and eliminate the threat," she countered.

"There were hundreds, thousands!"

"Keep your voice down!" she ordered.

He ran an exasperated hand through his messy hair and exhaled slowly.

"This is more than we can ask of you," I said.

"We're no longer doing this for you. We're doing this because they cannot survive. Why do you think they've grouped like this? Something is going to happen." Sibyl gave me a knowing glance.

"And we need to stop it," I agreed.

She nodded, looking away.

"So what do we do?" I asked, glancing up toward the sky. "The sun will rise in a couple hours."

"Well, sunlight would be the best time to attack, but—"

"But sunlight also is an issue on *our* end," I said. I still hadn't told Jasik that sunlight didn't hurt me, and I really didn't want to drop that bombshell now. Knowing that I had a chance at semi-normality, but I'd be giving it all up to be with him, was going to hurt him. I needed him to be thinking clearly, not worrying about our future as a couple. Besides, he already thought a hybrid would be better for me. I didn't want to give his argument any more grounding until I was able to *show* him just how important he was to me.

"Well, that's not entirely true, now is it?" My eyes widened at the realization of what she was about to do.

"What does she mean?" Jasik asked.

I bit my lip and faced him. I swallowed the knot in my throat.

"What is she talking about, Avah?" Jasik asked again.

I shook my head. "I'm sorry," I whispered. I glanced at Sebastian, who was nervously kicking the twigs at his feet, keeping his eyes lowered.

"For goddess sake, just tell him!" Sibyl said.

I opened my mouth to speak, but words were just out of reach. For so long, I was sure waiting to tell him was the right thing to do, but now, I felt ashamed. How could I have kept this from him? How could I lie to him after he repeatedly asked me if I was keeping something from him? He knew then, but I still did nothing. I felt sick, pathetic.

"Sunlight doesn't kill us, Jasik. You see, we're nothing like you. *She's* nothing like you." My breath caught as Sibyl spat her words at him.

Pain flashed across his face and lingered in his eyes.

"I'm sorry," I whispered. "I wanted to tell you. I just—"

"You kept this from me?" he asked, his voice low. "I asked you. I asked if you were keeping something from me. I gave you more than one chance to tell me. Why?"

"Because it doesn't matter! It doesn't change anything."

"This changes everything, Avah."

I shook my head, tears threatening to spill. "No. It doesn't. I still want to be with you." I stepped forward and reached for his hand, but he pulled away.

"Don't you see, Avah? You betrayed him with lies just as your witch coven had done to you," Sibyl said.

"Stay out of my head!" Jasik spat.

I inhaled sharply. "I didn't—I didn't mean…"

"Apple doesn't fall far from the forbidden tree, I see," Sibyl joked.

I spun on my heel to face her. "Shut up! Just stop! I know what you're doing, and it won't work. You won't break us apart."

She smiled. "Avah, you don't belong with someone like him. You belong with us."

"You seriously must be an idiot if you think I'd ever leave them to join you—especially after this!"

"Don't forget that you're not the only one who can see the future."

"I would never leave him for you," I said, my words coming in a whisper.

"You don't have to be the one doing the leaving."

I glanced back to Jasik. With arms crossed and head down, he kept his eyes from me. Pain etched his features, and darkness clouded his usually bright blue eyes.

"I was going to tell you. You have to believe that. I just didn't want *this* to happen. I know you. You think I deserve the world, but you don't understand that I don't want it. I don't want the sun or normal food or a regular life. *I just want you.* I want darkness and blood and a house full of vampires. Don't let this break us. Please."

He cleared his throat and looked up. In a flash, the pain was gone, replaced by a hard gaze.

"We should discuss a daytime attack. We're but four Hunters. You'd have a greater advantage during the day, without us, than at night, with us."

"Jasik, please." I stepped forward, reaching for him again. He backed away, putting several feet between us.

"This isn't the time, Avah. The sun will rise soon, and we need to plan our attack. We'll discuss this later, when we're alone."

I exhaled quickly and nodded. As much as I didn't want to wait, I also didn't like the fact that we were surrounded my eavesdropping vampires. I had gotten myself into this mess. I just hoped I could get myself out of it just as easily.

"There is an issue with this plan, though," Malik said, and Jasik nodded.

I met Malik's indifferent gaze. I wondered what he now saw when he looked at our future.

"Because even though you can go into sunlight, Amicia can't, and we're still outnumbered. This plan is placing quite a bit of faith on your hybrids," Jasik added.

"What happens when they realize the attack and do the only thing they can do: kill Amicia?" Malik asked.

I gasped. "You're right. I mean, that's what I'd do… if I were a crazy maniac. They're not complete idiots. They know we're here for her, and if they are put in a situation where they're going to face certain death, then they're going to take her—and us—with them."

"So our only option is a night attack: to sneak in or go with guns blazing," Sebastian said.

"We can only sneak for so long," I countered.

"True, but we'd get some for sure that way," Sebastian added.

My heart sank as his words hit home. He didn't expect to survive this. Glancing from one vampire to the next, I realized they all had doubts.

"We should sneak. Attack in groups. Stay secretive as long as we can, and then…" I wanted to say so many things then—pray we survive, hope we can kill them all, beg for Amicia's release—but Jasik finished my sentence.

"Go in with guns blazing?"

I nodded, meeting his eyes. There was softness there, but it didn't hide the pain that lingered.

"Do you see anything?" Sibyl asked Malik. Seers could only see their own futures—and the futures of those who affected their own. I doubted Sibyl could see our futures, because we weren't her people. If we didn't survive, she'd go on as if nothing happened.

He nodded but wouldn't meet her eyes. "I see death—both sides." The fact that he saw *something* meant he would survive this. That gave me hope. If he could survive, then all the Hunters could, too.

"We must sometimes make the ultimate sacrifice for the cause," she said without hesitation.

I blinked, staring at her coolness. "I suppose you've heard that before." The witches had said something painfully similar to me when I'd discovered I was the next chosen one.

She ignored my comment and walked away. "I'll find the others," she said over her shoulder before disappearing with Lillie and Jeremiah quietly in tow.

⁓

Our movements were slow, precise. We strived to alert no one to our presence as we stalked closer to our prize. We crept behind two Rogues, and in unison, Malik and I snapped their necks, twisting until their heads fell clean off.

Two down, I mouthed.

We stayed low, willing our movements to be steady, silent, though all the prayers in the world couldn't stop what was destined to occur. A twig snapped under my weight, and I froze, my heart beating so quickly I was surprised they hadn't heard it. A dozen sets of red irises were upon us; fangs lengthened and drool fell in steady streams.

I braced myself for the impact as Malik took a warrior's stance beside me. I glanced at him and was taken aback. The fear in his eyes was crippling.

"There's no one else I'd rather fight beside," I whispered. And it was completely true. I wouldn't want to fight—and likely die—beside Jasik, but I also didn't want to fight beside a stranger. I wanted to fight beside a worthy warrior, someone who loved me.

"Family," he said softly, his fist slamming against his chest in a show of love I'd only seen him bestow upon Jasik or Amicia. I was thankful to know my confession hadn't ruined the progress we'd been making, and I was hopeful that was because the seer in him knew Jasik and I would make it through this betrayal.

I put my game face on. When I faced them again, they were hurdling toward us. The ground vibrated with each foot's forceful impact. There were too many. We were outnumbered six to one, and I knew we'd never survive. Before he could move toward them, I reached over, grasping Malik's hand, ignoring his stiffness at my touch. Pulling at the power nestled deep within me, I threw my other arm out with a cry. My shield shook through my spine, expanding from within me until it blasted from my core. I focused all my energy on the shield and our attackers, watching it hurl into them. They were forced backward, flung effortlessly away, floating as if they were but a feather. I released Malik's arm and faltered.

With his steadying hand on my back, I said, "I'm fine." I gave him a reassuring smile even though I fought to slow my pulse and control my breath.

He smiled at me, giving me a thankful gaze, and then he was gone. By the time I found him, he was already upon the Rogues and had killed one. He took several hits before another fell. I was inexperienced without a blade, and my hesitation would get me killed. Calling upon my shield took too much time and energy, so I backtracked to something I knew well.

As a Rogue dashed before my eyes, I threw out my arms and called up fire. "*Incendia!*" I controlled the fire, expanding it to embrace two other Rogues before all three fell to ash.

Between Malik and I, we killed six Rogues. I was beginning to think we just might make it out of this battle alive. Malik and I stepped closer together, slipping back to back as more Rogues circled us like prey. This time, there were more than I had time to count.

I swallowed hard and said, "You take the ones on the right? I'll take the ones on the left?"

"Stay strong. We can do this." His voice didn't quiver like mine, as if he knew we'd survive this battle.

With hands by my sides and palms facing the sky, I formed a small fireball by calling upon the fire element. I bounced it up and down, slowly, tauntingly. Before I could reach within me and spray a stream of fire, the Rogues before me sparked in flames— one by one. A group of hybrids emerged from the trees as they fought to protect Malik and me from certain extinction. We didn't hesitate to make our next moves.

I showered a group of Rogues in flames and left them to burn as I aided Malik, who was cornered by three Rogues. I slammed my fist into one's back and yanked out his heart. I backhanded another, and as he fell, I jabbed my hand forward, snapping his neck. The head broke off on contact. Malik killed the final one and gave me a brief glance.

"Thought you could use some backup," I said with a wink. "Let's find our girl. We seem to be a good team."

He nodded once. In a motion too quick for my eyes, he grasped my arm and yanked me down. I toppled onto the ground beside him as a Rogue emerged from the shadows. She pounced on Malik, chomping her jaw like a hungry wolf as she leaned into his neck. I grabbed the back of her head, digging my fingers into her ratty hair, and yanked. She cried out as my fist made contact with her face, breaking her nose. Malik's hand dove into her chest and removed her still-beating heart.

"Holy fuck," I said, my heart pounding. "That was close."

"No more cockiness," he agreed.

I stood and somersaulted to the side as another Rogue attacked. He spun quickly and ran toward me. I threw my hand before me as I called upon air. The Rogue fought to reach me in the hurricane-like winds, but he was no match for my strength. His feet skidded backward until he slammed into a tree, where a conveniently broken branch pierced his heart. Malik stood before me, pulling me up by my arm.

"Let's go!" he called as he ran toward the huts. We searched each house, one by one, until, finally, we found her. Her body was broken and bruised. She was too weak to heal, to speak, to move. Dark circles coated her skin and under her eyes. She was sunken in the corner, her face bloody. Her condition made her too weak to even heal. Her skin was covered in both fresh and crusted bite marks. The fiends had just left her to die.

Malik scooped her up into his arms and returned to the door. My fangs lowered, and I offered her my dripping wrist.

"No!" Malik said, pulling away. My skin healed. "You need your strength to escape this. There are too many. We need to run. She can feed once we've found safety."

I nodded, and we emerged from the hut. The Rogues hadn't seen us get to her, and we could have run. No one would have noticed. Everyone was too busy fighting, surviving. There were body parts everywhere. Dead Rogues, dead hybrids; they coated the ground like missing puzzle pieces. Their blood splatter sprayed across the frozen ground like modern paintings. I searched the crowd for the Hunters. Jeremiah and Lillie fought effortlessly beside Sibyl. As I scanned for Jasik, my heart began to sink. The hybrids were running. I watched as countless retreated, finding safety in the woods. Facing hundreds, thousands of Rogues had been a death wish; we knew that, but we refused to face the facts aloud. I swallowed the knot in my throat and watched their retreating backs until they were no longer there.

"They're leaving," I whispered.

"I know. We need to go, too. I see the others. We need to get to them."

I nodded and raised my shield. We pushed past a group of Rogues, who each struck my shield with a force that shook me to my core. I fell three times, unable to stand the beating my shield was taking. I screamed in agony, not sure how many hits I could take.

"Avah! Focus on my voice. Ignore everything else," Malik ordered, and I obeyed. I stood on shaky legs, knowing that lowering my shield now, while we stood in the threshold of a few dozen Rogues, meant our deaths.

Slowly, we found our way to the other Hunters, and I enveloped them in my shield. Blood spurted from my mouth as I took more hits—these more forcefully executed. On my knees, I begged for the strength to survive. Strength I was sure wouldn't come. As my shield began to lighten and shake, Sibyl fell to her knees and grasped my hand in hers. Our power connected, and I felt her strength flow through me. The internal beating I was facing weakened, and my body began to heal. I stared at her, silently thanking her for saving me. Her eyes glowed a beautiful shade of neon violet, and I was sure my gaze, though awestruck, matched hers.

I stood, my legs still wobbly, and kept her hand firmly in mine. The Rogues slammed their fists against my shield, and I cringed at each contact. But I could push through. I would survive.

"We need to leave," Sibyl said, pulling me toward her.

I nodded and looked at the others, my heart stopping. "Where's Jasik? Sebastian?" I yelped, my voice shrieking unintentionally.

I spun around, searching the faces of our fallen but never finding his. Where was Jasik? Where was Sebastian?

"I saw them retreat," Sibyl explained, and I faced her. Her face was hard, unreadable. Could I trust her? I glanced at Malik; his questioning gaze meant he wondered the same.

"We know he's not here, so he's got to be out there," Lillie explained.

Jeremiah nodded. Both Hunters were growing weaker by the second. I gasped.

"The sun!" I looked up, searching the sky for any trace of lightness. In the far stretches of the earth, I could see the beginning stages of a glow. We didn't have a lot of time. "We have to find them before the sun!" I pointed to the sky for extra measure—*just* in case they forgot where the sun resided.

"Jasik is a strong fighter. He and Sebastian will be fine." Malik's voice came out harsh, strong. He gave me no reason to pause.

I nodded. "Let's go. Let's find them."

We ran at full speed. While some Rogues chased us, others stayed behind. We entered the woods, the safety of the trees providing minimal shade from the impending sun. When I could no longer hear the Rogues' footsteps, I dropped Sibyl's hand and lowered my shield in an attempt to conserve my energy. I was growing weaker by the second and knew we'd have to soon find both food and shelter. I canvassed the area as we sped to safety, but I found no signs of Sebastian or Jasik.

We came across a small clearing, and I spotted them. Sebastian, Jasik, and several hybrids fought off packs of Rogues. Without second thought, I ran toward them, determined to save my lover. But the look in his eyes stopped me dead in my tracks. He shook his head, glancing from me to Amicia. In a silent order, he told me to see her home. I ignored his command as I killed an approaching Rogue.

"Jasik wants us to go," Lillie said, stepping beside me.

"We can't leave him!"

"We must! He'll be fine. He has Sebastian and hybrids. They don't need us, but she does." She grabbed my arm, but I yanked it free.

"I will not leave him!"

Malik came to my side, Amicia now snuggly in Jeremiah's arms. "Go. Take her home. We'll find you," he said, looking at Lillie before grabbing my arm and pulling me toward his brother.

They were completely surrounded, but even so, every chance he got, Jasik looked at me, pleading with me to run. His eyes betrayed his secret: He feared my death—and the death of his brother—more than his own. He needed us tucked safely away in the manor, where Rogues, hopefully, wouldn't find us… again. With my eyes, I begged him to drop this. Worrying for me or Malik would only endanger him.

Malik had sprinted ahead of me, and I quickly joined him,

once again fighting by his side as we killed two more Rogues.

From behind, I felt something grab my neck. I spun, but the hand on my back was strong, stopping me short of a full circle. I now faced Malik, whose eyes widened as he fell limp, his neck broken. As I glanced back to see his attacker, the world went black.

CHAPTER
SIXTEEN

woke to the silence of my room. I was back in the manor, back safely in… I reached over, my arm brushing past the thin sheets. Jasik wasn't beside me. My mind was cloudy, the events hazing together. I sat up, my head lashing out in pain. My neck was stiff, too stiff. I could barely move. Slowly, I massaged the kinks that didn't seem to be there. I replayed yesterday's events in my mind, searching for answers.

And then I found them.

I remembered everything.

I jolted to my feet and stormed downstairs. The vampires of the house fell silent as I entered the room. I scanned the familiar faces until I found the Hunters. I stalked over and slammed my fist down against the table.

"What the fuck!" I ignored the shuffling feet behind me as the other vampires quickly left the room. I was furious.

Lillie glanced up at me, her eyes swollen and pink. "I didn't know," she whispered. "I thought—I thought," she hiccupped, "I was doing the right thing."

"In what screwed up reality would breaking my neck be the right thing?"

She shook her head, her gaze focused on the blood in her mug that she barely touched.

"Look at me!" I screamed, slamming my hand against the tabletop for extra measure.

"Avah, sit." Malik's voice was strained. I glanced at him with every intention of telling him he should be just as furious, but I lost my ability to speak. The pain in his eyes, the worry lines on his skin, the stubble on his jaw, his watery gaze… these were all signs of a Malik I had never seen before.

"W—Why?" I stuttered.

The world slowly began to suffocate me. I couldn't breathe, couldn't think. My heart sank so far it practically dragged across the wood floor.

"Jasik… He—He…"

"No!" I screamed. "No! Don't you dare. Don't you fucking dare!" Tears stung in my eyes, and I let them fall. I sank to my knees, my palms pressing against the cool ground, instinctively supporting my body when I couldn't. My chest heaved as I fought to control my spinning mind, my sputtering heart, and my clenching throat. The world was crashing down on me, and for once, I wanted it to.

"Breathe, Avah." Malik was kneeling before me, his hands firmly on my arms. "Breathe with me."

I shook my head, the tears falling in waterfall drips. He pulled me into his lap, and I leaned into the familiar frame, pushing my head against the crevice of his neck. Malik whispered into my ear, promises of how we'd be okay, how we'd get through this together, how we'd make this right. But I said nothing. Instead, I let it all go. I screamed, I convulsed, and I begged whoever was listening for one more chance. I offered my life in place of his, and I made promises I knew I'd never be able to keep. Malik's shirt quickly became drenched with evidence of my loss, and as my eyes dried, when my strength to produce more depleted, I noticed that he, too, was crying.

⁓

I woke in my bed, pressed tightly against a sleeping body. It was hard, muscular, unwavering. I moved closer, taking in his scent as

I curved against him. His arms were wrapped around me, and as I moved, they pulled me closer. His breathing hitched, and I knew he had woken.

I also knew it wasn't *him*. It would never be him.

Still, I wanted to pretend. I'd pretend for as long as he'd let me. I think he understood that, because he didn't pull away. Instead, he rubbed a hand through my hair, placing soft kisses against my temple, and my skin quickly grew damp with his tears.

How long could we mourn like this? We had forever, but surely, if a Rogue didn't kill us, a broken heart would.

I leaned against him, pushing myself up into a sitting position. The only movement he made was to wipe his tears away.

He sat up, wrapping his arms around me, as he pulled me into a suffocating hug. My breath caught, and for the first time in my life, I wanted to let it choke me. I couldn't imagine living a life without Jasik—but more, I couldn't imagine living an eternity while staring at the man who could have been his twin. I'd never seen their similarities before. But now, their lack of difference was smothering me.

Everything from the way he frowned, to the way he smelled, to the definition of his body, to the way his skin brushed against mine, to the way his breath hitched when I got too close... everything screamed Jasik, and the noise was deafening as I fought to regain control of my voice.

I let myself lean against him, resting my head on his shoulder. I didn't know what day it was or how long we'd been locked away in my bedroom, but I didn't care. We'd shut the world out, but it seemed fitting. The world turned its back on Jasik when he needed it most.

And then I remembered Sebastian.

I jerked back, gasping. Malik let me pull away, but he kept me in his arms, his hands settling at my hips. There was nothing erotic about his touch, but it screamed with a protective force. As much as my sanity would need to steer clear of Malik, I knew he wouldn't let me go. He would follow me wherever I ran. He would do whatever it took to keep me safe—Jasik's dying wish.

I swallowed down the lump in my throat and finally spoke.

"Sebastian…"

Malik tensed, his fingers digging painfully into my skin, but I didn't waver. I barely registered the movement.

"Sebastian was a," I shook my head, "*is* a hybrid. They're okay." I nodded, tears threatening to spill again. I wondered how many tears I could offer before my eyes dried up in their sockets.

He shook his head. "I've tried… I can't see them." His voice was soft, deep.

"You have to try again," I said with a squeak. I hiccupped as I took in a deep breath.

"I've told you," Malik said as he rubbed a hand across his buzzed head. "I *can't* see him!"

"There *has* to be something blocking you from seeing him. He isn't gone!" My voice shrieked as I screamed.

"My power has never failed me, Avah," Malik snapped, and I recoiled. Pain flashed across his face before he pulled me against him. I hugged him back as he whispered his apology.

"Don't you think we'd know? Don't you think we'd *feel* it or something? He can't be dead!" My voice was muffled as I pushed my face into the crevice of his neck.

"I need more to go on than that, Avah. I need more than a child's dream," he yelled. I pulled back, angered. I wiped at my tears. He exhaled slowly and released me as I slid off of him. I rested against the headboard, and he mirrored my move.

Closing my eyes, I pressed my index fingers against my temples, rubbing the pads in rough, slow circles. "Malik, you're not listening to me." I spoke softly, knowing he didn't mean to take his frustration out on me. This was hard on both of us, but to survive it, we needed each other. We couldn't let this separate us. "I don't think your power is failing you. I just think something is blocking you. A spell? Sebastian? A shield? I don't know… Stop focusing on *him*. Focus on *you*. What do you see in *your* future?"

"Why would that help us find Jasik?" His tone was harsh. I

turned toward him, and he wiped at his eyes.

"You once told me that the bond you share with your brother was so strong that your ability to foresee your future rubbed off on him. If his future affects yours that much, then you will likely see him in your future."

His eyes lit up as his gaze met mine. He closed his eyes, focusing on calling his power to foresee his future. Almost as soon as he closed them, though, they shot open. His face paled; his breath caught. He dug under the covers for my buried hand and grasped onto it when he found it. He closed his eyes again. I watched a shudder work its way through his tall frame. He dropped my hand, and his fingers dug into my arms. His eyes closed again, and I whimpered in response to the shock of pain sinking bone deep. His eyes opened, but they were glossed over, his mind deep in thought as he attempted to see my future.

"I can see my own future, Malik," I said, reminding him that, even though I may not have had the control he had, I was also a seer.

He opened his eyes, and my heart stopped as he returned my fearful gaze.

"I don't... I don't have a future. Neither of us do."

Malik's hands fell from my arms as he dropped his head.

I swallowed hard, our impending doom lingering heavily on me.

"How is this possible?" he asked, his head falling into his hands.

My earlier visions of death and destruction flashed before my eyes. Our war had only just begun, and we weren't going to survive.

∞

I stalked outside the manor. Somewhere inside, the vampires were both celebrating the return of Amicia and mourning the death of Jasik. I refused to play a part in Jasik's impending burial, because I refused to believe he was really gone. I reached back, grasping the handle of my seax, and quickly bounced down the front steps.

"Did you really think you could leave without me knowing it?" Malik asked as he stepped onto the porch behind me.

I didn't turn around. Instead, I ignored him and kept walking, hoping he'd just leave me be.

"Avah, stop!" he yelled.

I shook my head. "Just leave me alone, Malik."

I blinked, and he was before me, blocking my passage through the wrought iron gate that marked the edge of our property.

"Where are you going?"

"To find answers," I said defiantly, sidestepping him.

He reached out, intertwining our fingers as I tried to pull away. His grasp was painful, sending shock waves that tingled through me from fingers to toes. But I wouldn't acknowledge how raw I'd become. Not in front of him. Not anymore.

"Avah, please. Don't leave. Don't do this. You belong here."

"No, I don't," I whispered.

"I promised I'd keep you safe. I can't do that if you're not with me."

I brought my gaze up to meet his. His eyes were sunken and red. I was sure my face matched his.

"He'd want us to stay together."

"Stop!" I yelled, stepping back and yanking my hand from his. He reluctantly let go. I was sure it was only because I'd chosen to go a direction that led me farther away from the gate and closer to the manor's door. But I needed to get away from him. I could barely look at him. Touching him had become unbearable.

"Where are you going to go? There's nothing for you out there."

"I don't know. To Alaska. To find him, his body. And then maybe to Sibyl."

"Montana? That's where you want to be? With *them*?"

"Malik," I whispered before clearing my throat and speaking more forcefully. "I can't stay here. I can't be near you. You remind me too much—"

"Do you think you don't do the same?" he asked quietly. "Every time I look at you, I see him. I see your love for him reflected in your eyes. I see your pain, your loss. We're both mourning him, Avah. We need to do it together."

"Don't you get it? I want nothing to do with this—"

The faintest of heartbeats lingered in the air, but the smell of fresh blood was strong. It hit me in waves, rushing over me, cascading through my senses. My fangs lowered as my body alerted me to a smell I knew intimately. My breath caught, and I pushed past Malik.

"What?" he asked, his gaze following mine into the forest.

"It's him." I closed my eyes, inhaling deeply. "I smell him."

Malik exhaled sharply. "No, you don't. You're not well mentally or emotionally. You need to heal. Please, stay." He reached out, his fingertips sending shivers down my spine as he brushed against my skin. I shrugged him off.

Before he could stop me, I dashed past the gate and into the forest. My feet stomped against the hard-packed ground. I swatted at branches that hung too low, twigs cracking underneath my ungraceful jaunt. If Rogues lingered, they'd know exactly where I was, but I didn't care. Jasik was somewhere in these woods, and I needed to find him.

"Jasik!" I screamed as I pushed past overgrown trees. "Jasik! Where are you?"

"Avah!" My heart dropped, and I came to an abrupt stop, waiting for the next blessed word. "Avah!" I cursed as I realized it was Malik's voice.

I closed my eyes, focusing on my senses. I inhaled deeply, but his scent no longer wafted through the air. Had Malik been right? Was I just going crazy? I pushed the negative thoughts aside.

"Avah!" Malik called again, this time closer.

"Shut up!" I snapped as I tried to focus on my senses.

I heard him approach from behind.

"Don't ever just take off like that again!" he yelled.

"Malik, shut up! I can't concentrate. Stop breathing. Control your heart. Or go away!"

I knew I was acting ridiculous, but I also knew Jasik *was* out here. Somewhere. He needed me to find him, to bring him home.

I waited, listening as creatures of the night slithered around. I inhaled deeply, waving a hand by my nose as the salty sea air made me want to sneeze. I shook my body to relieve the tension and started again. Calling upon air, I increased the wind, hoping it was enough to bring his scent to me. When it hit me, it left no doubt in my mind that his bloody body was somewhere in these woods.

"Oh my goddess," Malik said, inhaling deeply as he stepped beside me.

"Let's go," I said as I ran toward the smell. I didn't stop running until the scent of blood coated the air in a hungry thickness. It wrapped around each breath I took, threatening to smother me with his delicious scent.

My hand found my mouth in a gasp as I took in the scene before me. In the center of a wavering shield, I watched as Sebastian and Jasik held onto each other. Their bodies were thin, bruised. Their muscular builds were now lanky. Slowly, they crawled, on hands and knees, in the direction of the manor, though I wasn't sure they actually knew where they were or how close they were to being home. Sebastian was too weak to maintain his shield. It lowered, and he reached over and sank his fangs into the wrist Jasik offered. Jasik cringed as Sebastian slowly drank from him. After only a few swallows, Sebastian brushed Jasik's wrist aside and brought his shield back up.

Malik and I both stared in dread at the scene before us. Unable to move, to speak, we watched it replay over and over. As soon as the shield faltered, exposing them, Sebastian drank just enough to bring it back up. Jasik's healing abilities were weak, but they were enough to bring them this far.

Swallowing back my tears, I dropped to the ground in front of them. I reached out, my hand grazing the shield's barrier. Ever so slightly, I pushed my palm against it. Sebastian cried out as though I'd hit him, and his shield fell. He was so weak. They both were so weak.

"Jasik?" I whispered. "Sebastian?" Tears burned behind my

eyes as I watched them. They didn't seem to register my voice.

Sebastian reached over to sink his fangs in Jasik's wrist, but I intercepted. I pushed Jasik's arm away, sitting between them. They rested beside me, eyes closed, chests heaving. Malik lowered himself behind me, rubbing his hands up and down the lengths of my arms. His forehead rested against the back of my neck, and wet tears drenched my skin.

"They're okay," I whispered, letting tears fall one final time.

I pulled Jasik into my arms, placing a soft kiss on his temple. He cringed on impact, my lips bruising his skin.

Malik and I sat with Jasik cradled in my arms and Sebastian in his. With tears streaming down our faces, we smiled at each other. We had done it. We had all survived. We had faced the impossible, and instead of staying when we knocked on death's door, we planted a burning paper bag of dog excrements and ran away.

It would take time and more blood than we had readily available to bring their strength back, but they were home, and they were safe—for now.

I knew something *was* coming for us, and there was a really good chance we weren't going to make it. But that was tomorrow's problem.

Tonight, I'd let go of the pain, I'd release the worry, and I'd welcome the darkness.

ACKNOWLEDGEMENTS

First and foremost, I'd like to thank my readers. I absolutely love being a writer, and I couldn't do what I love without you. You make this journey worth it. I hope you enjoy my stories as much as I do.

When I think about my recent writing accomplishments, I can't imagine being where I am without a select group of inspiring people:

To Tara, my wonderful editor—The only reason I can write these stories is because I know you're waiting there for me at the finish line. Whether I'm failing to find the right words or in need of wine and ranting, you're always there, even when I blow through a deadline. I appreciate you so much.

To Nadège, my book beautifier—I send you complete crap, and you make it pretty. I love you for that. You're such an amazingly beautiful inspiration, and I'm so grateful you're in my life.

To Patricia, Shawna, and Dallas, my writing cohorts—You're so incredibly inspiring. Thank you so much for always being there when I need to vent or set seemingly unreachable goals. I know I can always fall back on you ladies and laugh (or cry). I love you dearly.

To my family, my street team members, and my marketing team—You've been there since the beginning. You've waited patiently while I've lost myself in my writing cave. You've kept me on track. I wouldn't be where I am without you. Your support means more than I could ever put into words.

ABOUT THE AUTHOR

Danielle Rose is a writer of fiction and travel, as well as the owner of Narrative Ink Editing LLC. Danielle currently resides in the Midwest, where she spends her days at a local coffee shop planning her next vacation or plotting her next novel.

Danielle holds a Master of Fine Arts in creative writing from the University of Southern Maine's Stonecoast program. In addition to her Master of Fine Arts, she also holds a Bachelor of Arts in English and certification in professional writing from the University of Wisconsin—Parkside.

When not writing, traveling, or writing about traveling, Danielle enjoys being outdoors, cheering for her favorite football team (Go Packers!), and spending time with her husband and their furbabies: two dogs and a cat.

Visit Danielle online: www.Danielle-Rose.com.

57827879R00138

Made in the USA
Charleston, SC
23 June 2016